TRESPASSES

TRESPASSES

PAUL BAILEY

1817

Harper & Row, Publishers
New York and Evanston

FIRST U.S. EDITION

LIBRARY OF CONGRESS CATALOG CARD NUMBER: 77-123979

And it has been well believed through many ages that the beginning of compunction is the beginning of a new life; that the mind which sees itself blameless may be called dead in trespasses – in trespasses on the love of others, in trespasses on their weakness, in trespasses on all those great claims which are the image of our own need.

GEORGE ELIOT: *Felix Holt, The Radical*

For Elsa and Lila Brunelleschi

1

EARLY

It is May and the sun is shining. It is warm.

Early this morning, walking in the grounds, I stopped before an apple tree. I looked up at its branches, which seemed to droop under the weight of so much white and pink.

My head was empty; I could enjoy the blossom.

HER

She has been dead some weeks. Mrs Dinsdale complained – the state of her bathroom due to all that blood. People who disposed of themselves, she told me, were as inconsiderate as they were wicked. If wicked was putting it too strong, perhaps unnatural was nearer the mark. My wife had gone against nature.

PEACE

Endless green and blue: below and above. And one apple tree – white and pink, because it is always spring – darkening the earth, and fiercely light against the sky.

Some birds, occasionally singing, and a sun just strong enough to look into.

THEN

It was not a scream in the strict sense of the word. It was more like a howl.

BEFORE

Mrs Goacher, breathless, led me up. She stopped on each floor for a rest. She said, 'Christ Almighty, it gets worse every time. It's just as well I don't have a new tenant every week. You're not religious by any chance?'

I replied that I wasn't.

'That's good to hear. Not that I have anything against believers — except the one, that is — because I haven't. Me saying "Christ Almighty" didn't offend you, did it?'

'No.'

But I did not mean to write about Mrs Goacher, the mother of Mrs Dinsdale, whose bathroom Ellie had thoughtlessly untidied. I meant to describe that long, empty room, and how it was before either of us had lived in it. I shall try again some other time.

BLACK

Rain started as we moved towards the grave. Wind sent leaves in our direction: one settled on my sleeve, another in Mildred Harroway's hair.

My mother put a knuckle to her mouth.

Turning, I saw Miss Potter leave the chapel and walk away.

When we were home, drinking ports and brandies in the best room above the shop, Mildred Harroway said 'She had a nerve to come.'

My mother asked me to pass the biscuits round. Empty stomachs and strong drinks, she said, never did go well together.

HERE

I am numb again, content to record that a shower is flattening the bluebells beyond the gravel path. Soon, when the rain is finished, mist will rise up from the lawns. I shall open the windows, so that the sweet smells can fill the room.

BOY

I tried to break away from them. My father said 'Not so fast, Ralph. We have all day. The animals won't run off. Miss Potter wants to look at this tree.'

'We keep stopping. You two walk so slowly.'

'Do we, Ralph?' Miss Potter hadn't spoken to me before, merely smiled, showing teeth much whiter than my mother's.

'Yes, you do,' I said. 'It's only a tree.'

'But look at the blossom on it. Isn't it lovely? I think there's nothing lovelier in the world.'

Her cold right hand pressed my warm left one. I asked them to let me run to the gates. Only yards ahead were elephants, lions, bears, snakes.

They released me. I ran, my arms out like wings.

HER

Ellie's great cow's eyes stare at me. I look into her face and her lips part. I can see her word forming—'Why?' I am tired, thoroughly sick and tired, of answering her. I go to the window: a pigeon on a chimney pot gives the view some interest. Self-immolation, I wonder? I rack my brain for good reasons why a pigeon should sacrifice itself. It is no use: her silence finally intrudes upon my thoughts; there is no escape in childish speculation.

PLEAS

Let these pages speak for me.
Let me be fair to them, as I could not be before. Let me be just.

BOY

Some nights after the burial I awoke screaming. I'd been on an endless beach, pebble on pebble, dazzling white pebbles for miles. I'd made for the sea—there it was; it would cool me. Yet the more I advanced, the quicker it retreated. When I looked at the sky it changed to pebble. I stopped, scanned the vast landscape: nothing. I closed my eyes, sent my hands away from me to touch, to feel: nothing, no one. A word came, speaking to me in its own voice: Alone. It continued to speak, echoing along the pebbles.

I lay until dawn, almost demented. He would not come back. He was gone. Worse, *I* would never see him again. I tried to cry—my mother, hearing me, would come to the bed, perhaps kiss me, although it now embarrassed her to do so. Then I could blot out my worries in sleep. But it was impossible. A truth had come to me—there is a grief too terrible for tears to ease.

I went, the following evening, to Miss Potter's flat. I waited for half an hour on the landing before knocking at her door. She did not appear surprised to see me. She smiled and invited me to drink some coffee. We discussed her plants, when they bloomed, how they grew. She spoke slowly, thinking out each sentence carefully. She did not mention my father.

I left, hours later. She kissed me. She ruffled my hair, then apologized.

I ran down the stairs and along the street.

As my mother stirred the cocoa I realized that I had been happy.

HERE

The sunlight, blazing, does not aid my thoughts. I see dust in corners; how the walls are yellowing; where the ceiling dips. Nothing else is revealed to me. Today, instead of pain, I feel little more than a dull ache. My past refuses to haunt me. I am a thing, a shell.

I want desperately to discover that I am more than that.

ME

He was Mummy's Ralphie, his face scrubbed to a shine, each hair on his head beautifully in place.

Mummy's Ralphie looked down and saw his reflection in the tips of his shoes.

Mummy's Ralphie always left things as he found them, especially the lavatory, which Ralphie's Mummy called the toilet.

Mummy's Ralphie was good at his studies, and was top of his class in History, French and English. He could recite 'The Ancient Mariner' and 'Intimations of Immortality' and many shorter poems besides. Ralphie's Mummy was really proud of him, even though she did not like the look of poetry: it was funny — wasn't it? — putting words on a page like that. Mummy's

Ralphie was good in so many other ways. Although he never told her, Ralphie's Mummy could be sure in her heart that her spotless son did not go to the lavatories (toilets, toilets) on the far side of the playground when competitions were held to discover whose was the longest. Though the sneak once watched as some friends shook themselves to see who could shoot first, he left – he would have been pleased to tell her – before the victor was announced. In fact, Mummy's Ralphie was so thoroughly disgusted that he went straight to the wash-room and cleaned his face and hands in hot water.

US

We trod daisies underfoot. I tickled her most vulnerable spot, just above the ribs. She called me a bastard and ran away. I allowed her a good start, then chased her.

At the foot of the hill we stood together, breathing deeply, in fine rain. Ellie, pointing to an isolated cottage, said 'That's where they live. Now for the ordeal. Take heart.'

We walked, arms linked, until we sighted Mrs Chivers, who clutched the top of the wooden gate with both hands. Ellie ran from me again, to greet her mother.

Mother and daughter kissed. But when Ellie attempted to hug her, Mrs Chivers broke away suddenly, blushing. She said 'Let me meet your young man.'

'My mother, Ralph Hicks. Ralph Hicks, my mother.'

'Elspeth has written to me, mentioning you. Your father owned a shop?'

'He did. He was a newsagent.'

'Was he?'

I offered my hand to Mrs Chivers, who said, 'My husband, the Major, isn't here to welcome you, I'm afraid. You will see him later, possibly, before you go to bed.'

I pushed back my hair with the hand that had not been taken.

'You're rather a thin boy for my daughter to have chosen. She always rather fancied healthy individuals, a glow in their cheeks. Does he ride, Elspeth?'

'No, Mother.'

'He looks in need of exercise. Let's not stand here; let's go in and feed ourselves. Eat, drink and be merry. Can your young man fix Martinis, or does he only drink beer?'

'I drink both, Mrs Chivers,' I said.

'He looks very thoughtful, Elspeth. I hope he really isn't. I like a man to be straight as a die. I'm pleased to see he isn't wearing sandals.'

HIM

His first words were 'So you're Elspeth's intended, are you? Listen to me, calling her Elspeth. You're Ellie's intended?'

'Yes.'

'Forgive me staring at you, do please, but I can't believe our Ellie has actually caught a man in her net. You look real enough. Shall we indulge in a firm handshake?'

'Certainly.'

'As strong as you like, Ralph, I'm used to rough handling. Well, he *does* exist, Ellie, because I've just touched him. Love his eyes, Ellie, I really do. They smoulder. And I can tell from his high cheekbones that he spends his days scaling intellectual heights. I bet he's a right little Sherpa when it comes to learning, isn't he?'

'He is, Bernard, he is.'

'He's safe from me in that case. I never make passes at boys who take classes. I only lie down with absolute beasts, as I expect she's told you, Ralph.'

'She has.'

'As I thought. Our Ellie's never tongue-tied where my squalid habits are concerned. Anyway, my loves, let's not linger in this chilly hallway. Follow me. Mind your head on the chandelier, Ralph—it hangs low, like all the best things. Come into Auntie Bernard's palatial parlour.'

THEN

Julius Caesar and his bloody army entered the classroom, pulled the light bulbs from their sockets, disposed of the desks like so much undergrowth, hacked off the children's heads.

When it was over, everything quiet, I knew that the sound had left my throat.

BOY

Their voices interrupted my reading. I heard something like a sob. I went to the door, stepping lightly in case a board should creak.

My mother and Mrs Harroway were talking about men. Mr Harroway, I learned, had left his wife at the height of her feet trouble. He was a very physical man who hated illness. He had never been sick in his life and hadn't a blemish anywhere on him.

'He looked at my swollen ankles and said they turned his stomach.'

Then, she said, he donned his best suit—just casually, like it was a fine Sunday and he was all set for a stroll—and packed some shirts and underpants in a small suitcase (which was *her* property, anyway) and went and took a room in a boarding-house not far from the station. It had been rumoured—there was no truth to it, it was wicked gossip—that he'd gone there because of the widow who ran it. That was definitely a lie: was it likely that a man who had left his wife because of her feet going ugly would rush straight into the arms of a woman who had an unsightly birth-mark inches above her wrist?

My mother replied that it wasn't likely. Then, sobbing, she said 'George.'

As I entered the room Mrs Harroway, both hands clasped around my mother's, was saying 'Now, Mary. Now, Mary.'

Seeing me, she asked, 'You love your mother, don't you?' 'Yes.'

'Hear what he says, Mary. He loves you, like Charlie and Milly do me.'

'Come and sit with us, Ralphie.'

WARM

I was already on the stairs when Mrs Goacher—in her doorway, with a pink glow behind her—called out 'Do you drink, Mr Hicks?'

'Yes.'

'Would your poison happen to be gin?'

'Sometimes, yes.'

'Care to join me for a tipple then? I haven't got designs on you; you'll be quite safe. The truth is, I'm feeling a bit on the lonely side tonight, wanting company. Madam has left her poor old mother alone with the bottle—actually, dear, she doesn't know I've got one—and I've been sat here watching bloody television, hoping for someone nice like you to come in. So get down them stairs this minute.'

A single lamp, shaded pastel pink, lit the room.

'There should be time for two doubles apiece before the cow gets back.'

'Who's the cow?'

'Who else? My bloody daughter, bloody Ruby. Mrs Dinsdale to you.'

'Oh.'

I looked at the painting above the mantelpiece: an Oriental woman with a green face.

'She bought me that. That's the only reason it's on the wall, I can tell you. I think she bought it out of spite, because she knew it would clash with everything else in the room. I like rosy colours, always did. "Rosy means cosy" was my mother's motto, and it goes for me too. So what does my kind, thoughtful daughter buy me for Christmas, Mr Hicks? That monstrosity. The word *is* monstrosity, isn't it?'

'Yes. Why?'

'I ask because Ruby's for ever correcting me over the way I speak. She says I disgrace her.'

'Oh no.'

'Oh yes, dear. Oh yes. She's a terrible snob, Ruby is. You'd think her shit was scented soap, the way she carries on. Why are you standing?'

'There's a cat in the chair.'

'Push him off.' She clapped her hands. 'Off you go, Timmy sweetheart. Brush the fur off before you sit down, dear. That's something else she did to me. Well, not to me exactly, to *him*: that helpless little animal there. Had him attended to. "I don't want him passing water"—just like her, saying that; she'd never say a plain word for a plain deed—"I don't want him passing water on my landings, making the place smell nasty." "It's nature," I said to her. "You can't go against nature." "It's either that", she said, "or having him put down. Make your choice." Well, I couldn't spend the rest of my life with his death on my conscience, could I? Imagine yourself in my shoes for a minute—I mean, which evil would you have chosen? I *have* a heart, Mr Hicks: there's enough pain in the world without me adding to it, even to the putting-down of a cat. So Ruby won again, as she usually does. It hurts me, you know, when I think about it: cutting off a dumb creature's knackers just to please the whim of a house-proud bitch like my Ruby. I say she's house-proud, which she is, but the funny thing about it is that she has all the pride and I do all the work. That's life, as they say. Here's tonic for your gin, dear, if you want it. I take a little hot water with mine, like my old mother used to do.'

Then, leaning over me, her hand on my arm, she asked in a whisper 'Has she been up to your room yet?'

'Who?'

'Ruby.'

'No.'

'A word of warning to you then, Mr Hicks dear. She'll be up to see you before very long, you can be sure of that. I tell you what her favourite trick is. It's changing the light bulb. She gets up on a chair, wobbles about a bit and then she makes out she's going to fall. That's when she asks you to come to the rescue. You do. She thanks you. You help her off the chair, she presses her body against yours and nine times out of ten she manages — only God Almighty and she know how — to make her skirt ride up. And that's when you're supposed to notice that she hasn't got her knickers on. It's true, Mr Hicks. Word of honour. I followed her up once and watched her through the keyhole. I thought I'd warn you in advance so you could prepare yourself.'

'Thank you.'

'Don't thank me, dear. I consider it my duty. Ruby, you see, doesn't drink nor smoke. She doesn't have any of what I call normal vices. I give you one guess how she gets her pleasure.'

'Men?'

'Men. She eats them. Honesty compels me to say it, even though she is my flesh and blood. I was never like that — quite the reverse, as a matter of interest. She doesn't take after me. She can never have enough. You've seen how ever so genteel she is, haven't you? A right Lady Muck? Well, it's all show, all bloody show. She goes on heat worse than any dog when the fit's on her. She's doing it this very minute, I'll wager, with one of her so-called gentleman friends. She spent hours this afternoon beautifying herself, so it must be roll me over in the clover night tonight. Finished your gin?'

'Not yet.'

'She'll walk in here later on with that smile of hers at the corner of her mouth—I know what that expression means by now. She'll have that smell on her person, too—she fairly stinks of men afterwards. Do you know, Mr Hicks, if she put all the cocks she's ever had end to end, there'd be enough of them to fit a handrail round the world. Drink up, dear.'

HER

I see her face sometimes. Ants come out of her eyes.

BOY

I ran across the field, my arms out like wings. I climbed to the top of the oak, up and up and up, and rested there, sweating. The sky above me was cloudless.

But then I looked down. The green beneath the tree's many branches seemed remote and unattainable. I felt dizzy. I closed my eyes, clenched my teeth: the branch I sat on, moments ago so strong and firm beneath me, now seemed fragile, about to snap.

I screamed.

The fields around were empty. Harvest was over. It was conceivable that no one would pass for days.

The blue above was as menacing as the green below.

I looked down again. Fear was an ugly emotion. It limited one. I had been confident going up; I should be confident going down. If I told myself often enough that it was not impossible, then it would not be so. My feet would find the right holds, and my hands.

In the farm later, in my room, after they had rescued me with ladders, I cried from shame.

HER

Her face as it was —

I see her pinning photographs to a wall. The first one in place, she stands back to look at it. A Sicilian woman sits in front of a desolate shack, her face refusing to give expression to any more grief.

She goes to the wall again. This time it's an African child, his eyes far bigger than Ellie's, his stomach distended, his legs mere sticks.

I ask her why she has put them up.

'As reminders.'

'They don't really mingle — do they? — with the furniture.'

BOY

We sat by the fire one November evening. My mother sighed and broke our long silence by saying 'The doctors cut into her head. Poor Milly.'

We looked at each other.

'The street is full of Milly's operation.'

'Is it?'

'Well, naturally. Cases of Parkinson's are rare.'

'I suppose they are.'

'It's an affliction more than an illness.' She repeated, without relish, her new word: 'An affliction, Ralphie. An affliction.'

The doctors — she had it on Charlie Harroway's authority — had first of all shaved poor Milly's hair. Every last lock of it. Then they'd cut in. They had a simple reason for cutting in: if Milly was ever to function normally again two particular nerves had to be separated.

'Which is what they've done.'

'Is it?'

'Yes, Ralphie.'

My mother's voice was flat and colourless, the easiest in the world not to listen to. But her face as she spoke was surprisingly animated. Her eyes glowed. The tip of her little nose twitched. Since my father's death she no longer cried as she'd once done, copiously, on the slightest excuse: the amount of housework, or the thought or mention of Miss Potter. Only the sufferings of others brought expression to her features now: her little nose, I remember thinking fancifully, scenting out interesting disasters. Milly's terrible affliction was the reason for her present liveliness.

'Mrs Harroway and Charlie are still at the hospital. They won't leave, they said, until they know she's better.'

'Where will they sleep?'

She ignored the question.

'They're both afraid, they said, she'll stay bald. The doctors warned them of the risk. And they warned Milly, naturally. I think it's so brave of her.'

'Yes, Mother.'

We said no more until it was time for bed.

HIM

'But you *must* have loved someone.'

'Only my poor white-headed mother, Ellie. Only her.'

'I meant a man.'

'I know what you meant. No, I've never loved another man.'

'Why not?'

'Ellie lovely, you and your questions, you're worse than the bloody Inquisition. How do I know? Because I never have. I'm not cut out for the devotional stuff.'

'You should be.'

'Ellie dear, dear Ellie, you do talk balls. Why should I be?'

'Well, you should, because—'

'Because?'

'Because, without love, life is senseless.'

'Senseless it may be, Ellie, but I'm here to tell you it's fun.'

'Fun? Only five minutes ago, over dinner, you were telling us how you were beaten up last week.'

'Oh, that was just to aid your digestion. Anyway, it was the first time I'd been thoroughly molested in two years. He merely left me winded, if a trifle bruised. I faked it up, as I so amusingly related, with a selection of my best operatic screams, and he flew out of here long before the grievous bodily harm stage was reached.'

'Must you always joke?'

'Yes, dear, I must.'

'I mean, one day it could be serious. I mean, you could be –'

'I know what I could be, Ellie, and I'm quite prepared for it, so clear your mind of all worry. Precautions have been taken. There's a fatal overdose by my bedside, ready to hand.'

'But why?'

'Yet another question. Cover her mouth with plaster, will you, Ralph love? To kill myself is why. The idea far from appalls me.'

BLACK

Rain softened the two heaps of earth and trickled down into the hole. The parson quickened his speech. Mud, rather than dust, descended on the coffin.

I followed my mother and Mrs Harroway into the car. Mr Poole, the undertaker, held the door open. He apologized for the English climate spoiling an otherwise perfect occasion, but there you were, you couldn't order God to make the sun shine or the clouds hold – not even the best funeral parlour south of the river could manage that.

My mother smiled as she accepted his handshake.

At least, he continued, there had been time to arrange things, to summon relatives, to allow the nearest and dearest a parting glimpse. In Egypt, where he'd been during the war, and in all the hot parts of the world, a burial had to be a heartless business, over and done with in a day or so because of the danger of the flesh turning nasty in the heat.

'I have a nice spread laid out at home, Mr Poole. A joint of ham and some cucumber rolls and plenty of biscuits and drink, of course. Do join us if you have a moment.'

He said he would. He could indeed spare a moment from the office. He wasn't snowed under with work, it being August still and not much call. He would be delighted to come along.

'Brandy's as good as a medicine on a day like this,' said Mrs Harroway.

AFTER

The fog stayed with me as I went down the stairs, eyes open or shut. It thickened with every step my feet took for me.

At last I saw, through the red I was drowning in, a darker shape. I stopped and it came towards me, largening, widening.

When it was near I clutched at it.

'Bath.'

The word miraculously out, the shape left my fingers and the floor was beneath me, smelling of lavender.

PEACE

Thrushes woke me, shortly after dawn. I left the bed – on top of which, fully dressed, I had fallen asleep last night – and went to the window. I rubbed my eyelids and blinked several times. There was my perfect scene – earth, tree, sky – forming in front of me, in patches, as the mist cleared.

WARM

'Accept these as by way of congratulations, Mr Hicks dear. They're only violets, only a small token, but it's all I can afford until Madam obliges with the weekly allowance.'

'You're kind, Mrs Goacher.'

'I'm glad you're taking a wife, Mr Hicks dear, I really am. It's one in the eye for her, all right. Ruby, you see, was under the impression you were pansy. She wouldn't tell me why but I had a good guess. It was because you didn't respond, wasn't it? To her mating-call?'

'Yes.'

'Underneath the lamplight?'

'Yes.'

'Yes. I had a feeling I'd guessed correctly.'

HER

'They said you screamed. They were frightened. They could see no reason. Ralph, I want you to tell me. This morning, Ralph, there was nothing the matter.'

'This omelette is terrible. I've just swallowed a piece of shell.'

'Why did it happen?'

'Omelettes are simple enough things to make. You break the eggs, you whisk the yolks about a bit, you—'

'Why, Ralph?'

'I can't eat any more of this. What's to follow?'

'I'll fetch it.'

'Thank you. Some more wine?'

'No. Not for me.'

'More for Ralph then.'

'It's a rice pudding.'

'So I see.'

'Is that enough for you?'

'Ample.'

We ate in silence.

'You won't answer my questions?'

'What did you say?'

'Will you answer my questions?'

'There was only one. You asked why. The answer's easy. I don't know.'

'But you must.'

'But I don't.'

'It was as if you'd gone mad. They said.'

'They were right.'

'Were they misbehaving? Were they rude?'

'They were most attentive.'

'Then why?'

'I told you.'

BOY

My father called me into the shade.

'Sit a moment, Ralph boy, and listen. I don't wish to sound like your mother' — he smiled at me; I smiled back — 'but I want you to put your shirt on again and to do up some of the buttons, and to run this comb through your hair. We're going to meet a friend of mine. Her name's Miss Potter. Once we've met her we'll all go on to the zoo together. Will you promise me something?'

'Yes.'

'Will you promise me not to mention Miss Potter to your mother?'

'Yes.'

'You'll like her. She will take to you.'

HERE

I am sick of myself. I am so truly sick of myself.

HIM

'I said to him, dears, "Look," I said—Christ, I sound like a charwoman—'

'What did you say to him, Bernard?'

'Are you on tenterhooks then, Ellie? Well, I told him, in the fewest and choicest words that my startled brain could muster at the time, to pay me a visit as soon as he was cured. The nerve of it! And the sheer bloody arrogance, too. "Employ your wrist," I said, "if you're *that* frustrated, but kindly keep your diseases to yourself." He was so calm about it, loves, telling me that one shot of penicillin would put me straight should I be unlucky enough et cetera. Well, I informed him that my days of being poked about in the subterranean passages of one of our grim Victorian hospitals were well and truly over. I've had quite enough of those dwarfs shining their torches up me, I can tell you. Did you know that practically every clap clinic in London has a dwarf in attendance?'

'I didn't actually. Did you, Ralph?'

'No.'

'It's true. In my experience it is, anyway. Funny little garden gnomes in white coats. Very sinister, they are, very Wagnerian. Not, I hasten to add, that I've visited all the clinics in the great metropolis—'

'No?'

'No. Only the ones within a ten-mile radius. Though I was in a French one once. Many, many moons ago when I was young and lovely. I was on holiday with Mums and I got a dose in the front—the only time, I might add—from a chorus boy with liquid eyes. God, when I think how I suffered. This, you see, was just before the war, and the French method of curing you was primitive to say the least. I was given, my loves, an instrument like a water-pistol. Yes, I swear it, you're not to laugh. And I had to shoot warm water into my organ twice a day for weeks on end. I fainted the first time, right out, and when I came round, I remember, I put my hands together and said a prayer because I was so relieved that Mums hadn't walked in and discovered me on the floor with my parts hanging out and a gun in my hand. I was very ashamed of myself, hag-ridden with guilt to tell the truth, and I was terrified all the time that Mums would find the pistol and start asking questions.'

'And did she?'

'No. I told her about it, years afterwards, when we were drunk together one night. She laughed so much I thought she would have a seizure.'

PEACE

A green field and a blue sky and a tree in blossom.

BOY

A leopard cub bit its mother's tail. Three gibbons flung themselves into the air in one movement. A rhino slept on its side.

What with the chattering and the little old faces, the monkeys are very like us, people said.

Miss Potter laughed and told me to look. I looked. A sparrow was pecking at the lion's meat.

US

'I was awfully bloody unfair to them, wasn't I?'

'To whom, Elspeth?'

'My parents. This afternoon. When I told you about them. I made them sound caricatures, didn't I? Monsters. Would you have guessed from the way I spoke that I really love them?'

'Yes.'

'Be honest with me, please. What I mean is, Ralph, is that it turns my heart over, the way they behave.'

As I kicked the quilt from the bed I wondered if I was mad as well as drunk. Why should I involve myself with Miss Elspeth Chivers? She wasn't even a beauty: her breasts and hips were large.

'Don't cry any more,' I said, and my gentleness surprised me.

HIM

'Ralph Hicks.'

'I know who it is.'

'Bernard?'

'None other. And you don't need to ask me if I've heard the news because I have.'

'Oh.'

'Is that all you can say?'

'Yes.'

'You fucking cold fish. You iceberg. May you rot in hell for what you've done.'

'Thank you.'

'It's a pleasure. May I end by saying that "cunt" is too good a word for what you are.'

'You won't have me crawling, if that's what's in your little mind.'

I sat up and listened. His words came out evenly, at their usual steady rate, although he was as near to shouting as I had ever heard.

He went on: 'And don't think that by keeping on with your crying that you'll get my pity. You won't. You can sob till your ribs ache from the effort. Can you hear what I say or do you want me in more of a temper?'

'I can hear you,' she said. 'And so can the whole street.'

'You mean the bloody Harroways? And the bloody Dacres on the other side? Is that all that worries you, that those narrow-gutted friends of yours can hear me giving you the truth?'

'Ralphie will hear you too. You know he will. He sleeps light.'

'Let him hear. Let him judge.'

'I don't want him to—'

'Yes, you do. You want him to hear your bloody snivelling and to take pity. That's what's in your little mind. You want him to know what a martyr you are.'

'I don't. I don't.'

'I say you do.'

'You say!'

'I say. I know. I know you well enough, Mary Longhurst.'

'My name's Hicks. I married you. My name is Hicks.'

BEFORE

I saw the room and my heart leapt. It was so large and long and so much light streamed in.

Mrs Goacher said it was more like a flat than an ordinary room. A painter, a scruffy type in plimsolls, had once used it as a studio. A funny bugger, who now lived on a farm in France. She could just see the useless article coping with cows and goats and all sorts. If his pictures were any indication, he wouldn't be able to tell one end of the bull from the other. I walked through both blocks of sunlight and opened a door.

'I wouldn't try swinging a cat in there.'

It was a small kitchen with an ancient gas stove and a cracked china sink.

'What will you do for furniture?' she asked.

I replied that I had a bed and a desk and some shelves with books.

'You'll lose yourself in here,' she said.

That, I wanted to tell her, was precisely my intention.

BOY

The whole street was there. After all, it was an occasion. It wasn't likely that Charlie Harroway would get married again. He'd waited forty-two years before taking the plunge, so you could be as sure as you ever were of anything in this world that he wasn't making a mistake: he'd found the right girl in Joyce Edmonds. Joyce was no oil painting, everyone in the district who knew her agreed, her bones were far too big for prettiness, but then Charlie himself was not on the handsome side either: when his jacket was undone you could see the beginning of a drinker's tummy and what a strain it was on his top trouser buttons.

The church, which was usually occupied only by the few old faithfuls, was filled to bursting with half the neighbourhood and members of the Harroway family—some of whom, Mrs Harroway was heard to say, she herself had never seen before and, if looks were anything to go by, she hoped she wouldn't have to see again. If Milly ever married, they would forget to send a round dozen invitations at the very least.

It was a white ceremony of course. Every bride—said Mrs Yelverton, who never missed a wedding if it was within walking distance – somehow looks beautiful on her day of days, no matter how plain. And Joyce was no exception. It was sad when you thought about it, that some poor girls only looked radiant for one solitary day out of their entire lives.

And then the cars took everyone – everyone of importance, that is – on to the Jubilee Hall, where Mr Ansell, the caretaker, must have worked like a black for nights on end. The floral arrangements took the breath away and it was a wonder the tables didn't collapse under the weight of food.

But before they attacked the pork and beef and ham and chicken, a little silence was requested. Yes, it was business before pleasure: they had to listen to some speech-making first. And the cards and telegrams had to be read out, too – this was Billy Booth's pleasant task, since he was Charlie's best man and oldest friend. Billy amused all and sundry by remarking that they could partake of a drop of bubbly by way of a toast (or plain old beer, if they were too common to appreciate the flavour) but would they please keep their thieving hands away from the grub until he personally gave the starting signal? Billy made many other jokes in his long tribute to Charlie – some of them, it was thought, a bit near the knuckle considering the vicar and his lady were present. He ended by saying that although Charlie was a wild boy he was sure that Joyce wouldn't have any trouble taming him: she came of good country stock and had a strong pair of fists on her.

When the laughter was done, it was time for the messages and greetings. Billy had read quite a number before he pretended to wipe the sweat from his brow – the effort was killing him, he said. Most of the cards and telegrams were just sincere good wishes and hopes for future happiness, but one or two were really droll – the bride's father, who was a wily old fellow, had sent a corkscrew by registered post. The label attached to it read 'In case of emergency'. Mrs Edmonds gave her husband a playful slap on the back of his hand, and more than a few glances were cast in the vicar's direction.

But it was Mr Poole's telegram that won the most approval –

it was funny, but then it was sweet as well. It was in the form of a poem: 'Charlie the captain, Joyce the mate, Crew to follow at a later date.' Who would have credited Mr Poole with a sense of humour, a man who earned his livelihood in that grim job?

The band arrived at seven, but it was quite a while before many people could summon the energy to step out on to the floor. For the first six dances, it was only the youngest who ventured forth—everyone else, including the newly-weds, was much too winded. But, round about nine, the older folk were well and truly on their feet again, waltzing and even jiving, putting the youngsters themselves to shame. At midnight balloons were dropped on the dancers, some of whom were complete strangers who had strolled in from the pub nearby. The drunkest was plainly Irish.

Each guest in turn thanked Charlie and Joyce most gratefully and hoped the weather would stay fine for their fortnight by the sea. It was a pity about Milly walking out as she did, it must have been the drink or it could be jealousy, it was difficult to know with some women. It was also a pity about Mrs Hicks's boy, such a snob for his age, sitting by the wall all night with a sneering expression on his face. It was unnatural to be so gloomy. He'd come near to spoiling a perfect celebration with his moodiness.

HER

Someone—it might have been the coroner—read out the note in a flat voice.

'Ralph. I would rather be dead than live with your contempt. I am sick with love of you. Elspeth.'

I remember I scratched my chin. It was something to do.

HERE

I still see pebbles – miles of them, dazzling. I realized, this morning, that I had been on the beach again. I had had a monkey for company – it pranced, it jumped and it licked its tail.

BOY

Grandmother Longhurst said, 'The boy's at the door, Mary.'

My mother turned quickly. 'Go away, Ralphie. Go away this minute.' She wiped both sweat and tears from her face with the edge of her apron. 'Please, please, go away.'

I asked them what they were doing.

My mother stared back at me, open-mouthed. Her lips came together once, twice. A sudden flurry of chickens outside finally brought words from her.

'Oh – nothing,' she said, above the din.

'What a fool I have for a daughter, telling the boy it's nothing when he can see it's something with his own two eyes. It's your grandad we've got here.'

'You told me he'd gone to London,' I said to my mother.

'He's gone a sight further than that. He's in Kingdom Come, Ralph. He's dead. Take a peep at him if you want.'

'No, Mam, no,' said my mother from behind her apron.

'Do you want him to grow up soft? Calm yourself, Mary – you're in more of a state about Albert's going than I am myself. You don't want a little jelly for a son, do you? You can't protect him from life for ever, you know. Come over here, Ralph, and put a step on it – take your look and then be gone with you.'

I stood next to my grandmother by the bed.

'Someone's stolen his teeth.'

'No, they haven't. I've got them. Your grandfather's going back to his Maker the way he came.'

'But what are you doing with him?'

'What does it look as if we're doing? There aren't many tricks you can get up to with soap and water. We're making him sweet for his box. Now go and play.'

'Yes, Ralphie, go and play.'

My grandmother called me back from the passage.

'I've a question to put to you, my lad, and I want a straight answer. Did you piddle your bed last night?'

'No, Gran.'

'Good. You're getting better. You might find some gooseberry tart on your plate this evening.'

WARM

I was to remove the cat from the chair and make myself comfortable. I would have a gin and tonic in my hands in a couple of shakes. I could stay for as long as I wanted because tonight was another of Madam's nights.

'It must be somebody really high and mighty judging by the preparations. I've rarely known her be quite as thorough as she was today — nothing was overlooked. And then she had the gall to tell me just before she was leaving that she was off to see that new Biblical film that's on at the Palace. I could have spit, if I hadn't wanted to laugh. She must think I'm a bloody half-wit, she must. I got my spoke in though, Mr Hicks dear. I made my face come over all innocent and I said to her, "Feeling in a religious mood are you, Ruby love?" "Yes, Mum," she says right back without so much as a blush. "Well," I said, "I hope He appreciates all you've done for Him." "I don't follow you," she says. "I mean", I said, "I hope He appreciates how lovely you've made yourself." "Who's He?" she says. "Him. God." "I still don't follow you, Mum," she says and sweeps off, leaving her trail of scent behind her.'

We laughed. Breathing thickly, she lowered herself into the sofa. I broke a long silence by asking her about Mr Dinsdale:

what kind of man had he been? Had he and Ruby been happy together?

'He came from the north, Mr Hicks. He was a nice little man in many ways. He had a sunk-in chest and a Hitler moustache – not God's gift to women by any stretch. Ruby came home one night to our old place in the Walworth Road saying how she'd met this lovely gentleman and how he'd proposed to her after only two hours in her company. It seemed he'd come to the office where she was working at the time as a typist – I will say that for her, she knew her stuff when it came to shorthand and typing – and he hadn't been able to keep his eyes off her all the while he was doing business. He took her out to dine as soon as she'd finished working and then, just like that, he popped the question. Anyway, when she finally stopped talking, I said to her that I wanted to see him. She looked at me for a good minute as though I was a nasty stink under her nose, and then she said – she was stuck-up even in those days – that she wasn't bringing no gentleman into this dirty dump. We set to and had a blinding row after that remark – what was fine enough for her poor dear departed father and me was fine enough for her, I reminded her, and she could just push off if that was how she felt. The ingratitude! We spoke no more for five whole days, and then she waltzes in one night with the great man himself – five foot nothing in his socks, he was – creeping up behind her. A fortnight after they was man and wife.'

She needed to wet her tongue before going on. She did so.

'He was cagey, was Ernest Dinsdale. The sort of man you couldn't properly get the measure of. You've come across the type?'

I said I had.

'A bit of a mystery. He'd say one thing and you knew he was meaning another. It came as quite a big surprise to Ruby – and to me – when she discovered how well-off he was. He'd had this firm when he was younger – bicycles, I think it was – which he sold, and all the money he got from it he bought stocks and shares with. A tidy pile, Mr. Hicks dear, oh yes. He owned this house, you see—Ruby would never have earned enough to warrant a place like this. He left her everything he had.'

I repeated my question: Were they happy together?

'That I wouldn't care to say. I wouldn't swear to it. Of course, I never lived with them. I stayed down the Walworth Road. I only come here after he'd croaked. All I can tell you for certain is that they didn't argue much; they didn't fight like most married couples. She maintained, once he'd snuffed it and after she'd heard how much she was worth, that she'd loved him with everything in her—or some such tripe; that he was a man in a million. You would have thought, to hear her, that the sun had shone out of his arse. How she missed him, how she loved him! I don't think, between ourselves, she did. It isn't in her. She's never felt anything that I'd call love. She went where the money was and little Ernest had it.'

I filled our glasses.

'But as to happiness—well, Mr Hicks dear, who's to say? I don't think he had love in him either—not like Mr Goacher had for me, and me for him. He was polite and he respected me. He told me once there was no woman on this earth more precious than a mother. He always handed me a pound note, very discreet, whenever I visited. What he saw in Ruby was very simple and a bit strange if you allow your mind to dwell on it: he went for her bosom, I'm sure he did. You've seen yourself how large it is. I only found this out when he was a goner. We went through all his papers and belongings, naturally, and we found this drawer in an old sideboard in the cellar. It was jammed tight with photos and they were all of tits. Some had faces, I grant you, and there was a couple of below stairs ones, but it was that part of the body in the main. Ruby well nigh had a fit. She told me to go upstairs; she'd cope with the stuff, she said. He even had snaps of darkies—jungle women with knockers down to their bellies. No wonder, I thought to myself, his ticker was so weak; no wonder he died when he was barely past fifty. Tit, I should say, was Ernest Dinsdale's downfall.'

HER

'I could go to live with Bernard.'

'That will be nice and cosy. Girls together.'

'You bastard. If you had to live the way he has to—'

'I don't have to live the way he has to. I'm sorry, Ellie. I can't help being normal. Nor am I Jewish, black, blind, deaf, dumb, crippled, diseased. What an orgy of sympathy you could indulge in if I were.'

'What use are you to anyone?' she shouted.

'None whatsoever.'

'You're not human.'

'I dare say you are right,' I said. I left her, shaking, in the room.

ME

Mummy's Ralphie prospered. Mummy's Ralphie thrived.

Reading and writing weren't simply tasks as they were for all the other boys: with Mummy's Ralphie they were a passion. They consumed him.

Ralphie's Mummy spoke of her son with pride. She thought his head would burst from all the knowledge crammed inside it. It worried her slightly, the way he never let up.

Mummy's Ralphie won so many prizes that on speech days Ralph Hicks seemed to be the only name that was called out.

HERE

It is surely possible to change, to grow.

BOY

I went again, as she had asked me to. I took her flowers.

When she went out to make the tea I wandered about her long room, opening books, touching plants. I would have such freedom one day.

With tea there were Garibaldi biscuits. I told her that my father had called them 'fly cemeteries', and she smiled.

Shadows had thickened, almost blotting out corners, before she turned on lights. She would bring in some sherry: I certainly deserved it after listening for so long. I told her I was content to listen.

My mother would faint, I said, if she could see me drinking.

'She would faint twice over if she knew you were drinking with me.'

She handed me a second glass and reminded me of my age, and the likely consequences if I continued to live in this depraved manner. If I ate the plate of cheese provided, I would suffer no giddiness.

As we were friends now, and would remain so, it would please her to hear me address her as Laura.

'But I prefer you as Miss Potter,' I said, and blushed.

'I understand.'

THEN

Its echo stayed with me.

Then it was over, everything quiet, the children before me like figures on a frieze.

They came to life again with coughs and stares at each other and whispers.

One boy smiled.

'Oh, I approve of her. She's quite divine.'

We could still hear Mrs Goacher breathing with difficulty as she descended the stairs.

'I think she's a terrible old freak.'

'Ellie dear, where's your charity? I'm surprised at you.'

'It's such a performance, such an act. Every line she utters is aimed at the gallery. It's a wonder she doesn't wink, too.'

'She's too subtle.'

'Subtle!'

'Yes, dear. She's a polished artist. She has obviously spent years perfecting that little turn of hers. You saw how she warmed to me: she knew instinctively that she was meeting a kindred spirit.'

'Well, I'm sorry, Bernard, and I'm sorry, Ralph, but I think she's a monster. The way she talks about her daughter fills me with disgust. Ruby deserves her mother's pity, not her contempt.'

'Really, Ellie, you can't be so serious.'

'I'm afraid I can. I can't help it. It made me sick to see the two of you sniggering just now. Mrs Goacher is a cold-blooded fiend.'

'Fiends aren't usually so entertaining.'

'If you had a child, Bernard—'

'Dear heart, what a proposition—'

'*If* you had a child, Bernard, would you make fun of its deformity? You'd amuse your friends, would you, with all the gory details? I refuse to believe you could sink so low.'

'Ellie—'

'Ellie is going to the kitchen to prepare the salad.'

Her preparations soon began, noisily.

'I find Mrs Goacher a great comfort, Bernard,' I said. 'She's like a rock; she's there. She has no doubts. I feed her with questions and she always supplies the answer I expect.'

BOY

'Try and be warm to Milly, Ralphie. Make an effort now and then and be nice to her.'

'Yes, Mother.'

'Put your book down for a moment. Take a rest while you drink your coffee. And why don't you have the light on in here? It can't be doing your eyes any good.'

'No, Mother.'

'I was saying about Milly, wasn't I? The thing is, Ralphie, we must all of us rally round at the present time and offer her any help we can. She must feel lonely, now that Mrs Harroway's gone and not having anyone left to care for. It must cut into her. Milly is very proud, Ralphie, she will stand on her pride: I'm convinced that on her deathbed she won't find it in her to forgive Charlie for what he said to her on his wedding day. He's the last person she can turn to, whereas he should be the first.'

'Yes, Mother.'

'I shall offer her a job in the shop tomorrow. I could do with some assistance, and it will occupy her mind. You've enough work of your own, haven't you, with your studies?'

'Yes.'

'I thought so. I'll be off to the sitting-room then. I shan't disturb you any more this evening.'

US

We were cold. We huddled together.

Later on, she laughed. 'It isn't only the drink, is it?' she asked softly. 'I seem to have a virgin on top of me.'

'You have.'

'My lamb,' she said. 'My Ralph.'

She guided me in.

HERE

Impotent, I look around my room once more. I notice, for the first time, that a spider has decorated one yellowing corner. I want to be away from here, entering those lives I kept my distance from.

These fragments must speak – for me, for them.

BOY

'You can't expect the boy to rush into your arms, Mary. He hasn't seen you for nigh on six months. It's nothing to get in a state over.'

'Yes, Mam; I'm sure, Mam. He looks very well. You look very well, Ralphie. They say the war will end in a short while.'

'Who be "they" when they're out?'

'On the wireless. People on the wireless.'

'Let's hope they're right for once. What's that husband of yours up to?'

'He's in the Home Guard still.'

'He is, is he? Is he leading you a dance as ever?'

'No, Mam.'

'You wouldn't know if he was or not. You should have put your thumb on that one long ago, you should. Doesn't he want to see his son?'

'Yes, Mam, of course he does, naturally.'

'But it's me that's keeping him clear, isn't it? Come on, Mary – the truth for once.'

'Well, Mam, he doesn't really like you –'

'That's right. And the feeling's mutual.'

'I've told George many a time, as I've said to you, that he doesn't properly understand you.'

'Maybe he doesn't. But I understand him, Mary, through and through and make no mistake.'

'Open your presents, Ralphie.'

'Yes, lad. Open them. You're standing there like a tit in a trance. Don't you want to see what your loving father's sent you?'

US

'I hope you like him, Ralph.'

'I hope so.'

'What I mean is, he *is* the one person, apart from you, that I'm closest to. He's bound to behave frightfully tonight, he always does when he meets new people, and, I warn you, he'll go on about being queer as though he invented the condition. If he *is* awful, take it on trust from me that there's more to him than appears on the surface, won't you?'

I said I would.

'You must see him at work, Ralph, at the Institute. He's a different man then. You should see the enthusiasm he inspires in those Cockney boys and girls, it's astonishing, it really is. Oh Christ, we've gone past the stop. We must get off at the traffic lights and walk back.'

WARM

'As I say, Mr Hicks dear, I've nothing against believers—except the one, that is. And I wouldn't call him a proper believer, not like a Roman nor a Methodist, not in that class at all. No, he was one of those cranks, a real cracked nut I'd call him—he hung up these funny charts which he said helped him to prophesy the end of the world. I mean, I ask you, as if a scrap of paper could tell you something as big as that. Ruby asked him to leave in the end, after she found out how he spent his Sundays. Having a lodger who spoke at Marble Arch lowered the tone of the house, it was Madam's opinion. I had a private chuckle to myself when she come out with that, I always do when she puts on that ever-so voice of hers. She's a fine one, if anybody is, to talk of lowering the tone.'

I reminded her of her promise to tell me about the believer she had taken exception to.

'Oh, him, yes. Lavers, that was his name. Oswald—I think it was—Lavers. Well, the first time I saw him I was going out of that door there and he was coming down the stairs. No sooner had I wished him the time of day than he crossed himself. I tell you no lie. Anyhow, as he passed me, I tried to be friendly with him; I thought, being new to the house, that he might be partial to a little chat, so I mentioned to him that my bronchial trouble was playing me up again. He stared at me so long I thought he was trying to put me under his spell. Then, as calm as they come, he said "If you prayed to the Lord of Hosts you'd never suffer from aches and pains." After that, Mr Hicks dear, it was war between us for the rest of his stay. Do you want to hear how things came to a head?'

'If you have the time, Mrs Goacher,' I replied.

'For you, dear, yes, of course I have. They came to a head one night when Ruby was out and he obliged me with a call. He sat himself down in Timmy's chair without so much as a by your leave and started off by spouting the Bible at me. "I know my Good Book well enough, Mr Lavers," I said. "Well enough to do without your help, thank you." Which surprised him, I must say. Then he asked me—his eyes were on me all the while—whether I was aware of my daughter's inclinations. I caught him out good and proper: "Which ones?" I asked straight back. "The ones that are leading her into fornication," he said. I saw red at that point, Mr Hicks dear, and told him to watch his language. I asked him what exactly he was hinting at. I soon heard—that silly cow of a Ruby had gone to his room to see how strong his light bulb was and within minutes she was shoving her naked winker at him. And this silly bleeder, this bloody God-struck Lavers, was blaming me. Yes, me. Could

46

you credit it? I got off this sofa and I went across to the chair he was sat in and I told him that the late Mr Goacher had been the only man — *the only man* — to take his pleasure from my old bag of bones. I was a damned sight purer than my slut of a daughter, I said. When I'd done, I stood fuming above him. He got up ever so slow and crossed himself. "The sins of the fathers, Mrs Goacher," he said to me. "Remember them." I was lost for better words by that time so I shouted to him to piss off, which he did, I'm glad to say.'

HER

'She knew what she was doing, Mr Hicks.'
    'Yes?'
'She severed the main arteries.'
    'Yes?'
'Usually it's the wrists.'

BOY

It pained her, she said, not to know what I was going to do.
    She waited for me to speak. I drew a pattern on the table-cloth with my spoon.
    'I said it pains me, Ralphie. You should realize. You could tell me what plans you've made, if only for your father's sake.'
    'I've made no plans.'
    'You're teasing, aren't you?'
    'No, Mother.'
    'I hope you are, whatever you say.'
    I said again that I was not teasing.
    'You don't make sense to me. These days, Ralphie, I can't make any sense of you.'

'Why not?'

'I wish to God I knew.'

I looked at her. Her voice had not been so loud or so expressive for many years.

US

She lay sleeping. I left the bed.

Perhaps, I thought as I stood by the window, I shall grow into love.

I went into the kitchen.

Love, I hoped, would brighten my world. It wanted brightening.

I brewed coffee and took it to her. We kissed. I accepted her breasts as they were offered.

I entered without assistance.

We arrived at St Clement's with our arms linked.

HERE

Long before I returned to enemy territory for a Sunday visit I received a letter from my mother.

Dear Ralph,

It is not often you hear from me, although the other way round is the case as well. We seem to be out of touch. I hope you are well and your wife. Milly is well, apart from a chest cold that is, that had her laid up last week. My back is better. The two of us are very content in our little flat and grateful for the company we can give each other, we thank the Lord for such mercies.

The proper reason for writing is to let you know that

Miss Potter is dead. I thought you would be interested to learn. It was a quick cancer according to Mrs Dacre who saw the item in the local paper, over and done with in a fortnight. Galloping, is that the word Ralph or do you only use it for T.B.? It was all very sudden anyway. Whatever my feelings on the subject it was a terrible thing to happen.

I said to Milly that I thought I might go to the funeral but she told me no, I was not to, I was not to make a fool of myself. I said it would show some around this district that I harboured no grudge against the dead. But she said let those who want to think so think so but I was not to ruin my health. I was to consider my back and what the wind might do to it in that chilly graveyard. She was right as she always is, I can always depend on Milly. Write if you have news,

YOUR MOTHER

BOY

I sat in the park and wrote a poem. When it was safely down in the back of my French Grammar, I read it aloud. I did not understand it—the words had rushed from me, intent on release.

I write it down once more:

There is a wall too near me
And beyond it wailing
Sad nights old women
Scarred at a garden-end
Often or sometimes a growl
An unkempt lioness
Striding and striking
And if her long-mane glitters
There is a wall too near me.

Beyond its dark edge
Summer and spring
Fruit ripening singing
Laughter breaking and further
Night's reasons proclaim
And only a low sound
Marks where the cruel exercise.
There my wall begins
Where an animal crushed flowers
And ate and the long stalks
Not even perished.
There where they keep the sun
Is a wall and its deep side smothers
Being too near.

Why had I written it and how had it come? There were no walls near me — some plane trees, certainly, but in the distance.

Yet I was proud of my first poem. I copied it out and read it often.

THEN

One boy smiled.

HIM

'Hit me if you think I'm getting maudlin.'

I assured him he wasn't.

'Well, Ralph love, be very firm when I start to. Drink and Bernard Proctor aren't the best of companions sometimes. I have been known to be quite horribly tearful, I'm ashamed to report.'

Then very quietly, he said, 'I want to show you something, Ralph. It might help to make awful old me a trifle clearer to you.'

He unlocked a desk drawer and brought out an envelope. As he handed me a grubby card he asked, 'Can you make out what it is?'

At first I thought it was a German passport. It was obviously an official document of some kind. Then I noticed an English name—BURRIS, JAMES STANLEY—followed by several numbers.

'Of course you may know more about me already than you care to. Oh God, what am I trying to say? I'm as fraught as your wife tonight. Jim was my other half, dear, to coin a phrase, and that squalid piece of paper you're examining so intently was sent from a prisoner-of-war camp in Germany. He died there—it says so at the bottom. Oh, I'm sorry, Ralph—inflicting my Great Sorrow on you like this. I've nothing but contempt for people who do it to me. "I do not wish to hear," I say to them, ever so brusquely. It's just that I wanted you—and I promise I'll never bore you with the subject again—I wanted you, I suppose, to understand me a little better.'

He replaced the card in the envelope and returned it to the drawer.

Again very quietly, but this time with his back to me, he said, 'I wasn't always a parody pansy. I lived quite simply with Jim. I even spoke simply, which took some doing.' He turned to me. 'Hitting time is dangerously near, isn't it?'

'No.'

'Ralph Hicks, you lie. You're squirming, I can see. You're thinking that any minute now I'll be throwing my arms about you and collapsing in floods of tears. I shan't, have no fear. I have a sense of proportion about some things. And please, dear, whatever you do, don't mention tonight's little bit of undressing to Ellie, will you? I receive quite enough sympathy from that quarter as it is.'

US

The registrar's office was in a building next to the Municipal Baths. We could hear the swimmers' voices echoing.

'I never envisaged my daughter marrying in a place like this,' said Mrs Chivers loudly. 'It smells of lavatory cleaner.' She stared aghast as Mrs Goacher and Ruby entered, a floral spray across each satin bosom. Wordlessly, she indicated to her husband and sister — Ellie's Aunt Alex — that a little distance should be kept from the other guests. This they achieved by seating themselves at the back of the room.

I heard Mrs Goacher say that it had been her late son-in-law's view that there was nothing in this world more precious than a mother. She had known at a glance which of the ladies present was the one responsible for Mr Hicks.

After ten minutes we were man and wife.

HERE

I try to remember him. I try because I must put him together again. As soon as I have his face in my head the pebbles appear.

It seems I am left with nothing but my loss of him.

BOY

'You will come with me, Ralphie. I say you will come. To show respect, if for nothing else.'

'I don't want to show respect.'

'She was my mother.'

'I know she was.'

'Your grandmother —'

'That makes sense.'

I switched on the radio. My mother rose and turned it off.

'And what do you imagine they will think, the people in the village? When they see that you aren't with me? And what I will feel when they remark? It wouldn't hurt you to consider me.'

I hummed softly.

'I wonder sometimes if you are my son, I honestly do. It's your own flesh and blood they're putting in the earth on Tuesday, it's my Mam. Oh, Ralphie, the two of you were so happy when you stayed there, you loved your time on the farm. She scolded you, it's true, but then she scolded everyone. It wasn't so long ago, when you were growing, when you were staying there during the war, that I was worried myself, very worried, that you would be closer to her than you were to me. Or to your father.'

'I can easily look after myself for a few days. I shall fry eggs and bacon.'

'No, Ralphie. You'll come, I'm sure, like the good son you really are.'

'I won't, Mother. Just wait and see.'

'Do I have to plead with you?'

'I hope not.'

She could not acknowledge defeat until her last hand was played. 'Your father would be ashamed of you.'

'I can't speak for the dead, Mother, but I don't think he would. Father hated Grandmother Longhurst. And she hated him. She didn't come to London for his funeral.'

'She was old, Ralphie. The journey was too much of a strain for her.'

'She didn't come.'

'I can't believe you've had an education, to listen to you. You're childish, you are, Ralphie. You're worse than a boy. I'm glad I don't have brains, if that's what they do for you.'

In the morning she left for the country.

HER

Her cow's eyes stare.

'What is it?' she asks.

'What does it look like?' I reply.

'It's a screen.'

'That's right. Clever Ellie.'

'But why?'

'What do you mean?'

'What I mean is, Ralph: why did you buy it?'

'I liked it. It appealed to me. If you move nearer you can see the design on it. It's St George fighting the dragon.'

She moves nearer. She touches it—her hand comes forward, brushes against it. But then she withdraws her hand—quickly, decisively—as though afraid that the screen will bite it off.

'Ralph.' She smiles. 'You fool.'

'Am I?'

BOY

'Happy birthday, Ralph,' she said. 'It's only a month since you came here last and yet you look at least a foot taller.'

'My mother's always telling me I'm growing fast.'

'Is she? What's the matter with you? My arm is aching already from the effort of holding this door open for you. Aren't you coming in?'

'Yes. Yes.'

She laughed. 'Well, kindly do so.'

There it was: my freedom. The long room, the plants, the light.

She described her holiday in Cornwall—the hours on deserted beaches, the endless walks across wild countryside, the hundreds of kinds of birds that every day surprised her. The fern by the window would act as a souvenir of a blissful fortnight.

'My apologies to you, Ralph. Holidays make bores of the best of us, don't they? And on your birthday, which makes it worse. I have a present for you.'

It was a book: an expensive edition of La Fontaine. For as far back as she could remember she had found him very wise and very funny.

I wandered while she prepared the tea.

'I have some whisky, Ralph,' she said, soon after the shadows deepened. 'I bought it, as charladies say, for medicinal reasons. Would you prefer it to sherry now that you're a grown man of sixteen?'

It burned me pleasantly, all the way down from my throat to my stomach. It soothed the pain from the tooth that a lemon biscuit had set on edge.

And it gave me courage. Courage to leave the chair, to stand for a moment with my feet apart, to move towards her. I have courage, I thought, as I neared the settee where Miss Potter with the shiny white skin and the long red hair was lounging so comfortably. 'Faint heart'—someone, probably no less a person than Shakespeare, had said—'never won fair lady.' My heart was no longer faint. It was expanding. It was commanding me to kiss her white skin, to stroke her red hair.

She smiled up at me. Her teeth, which I could see were real, were still whiter than my mother's.

I steadied myself. To fall on her would be rude. It would be graceless. I leaned over, one hand on the settee's arm preventing me from falling. 'I love you,' I said.

'No, Ralph.'

'I want your love.'

'No, you don't.' Her face came up to mine. 'No, you do not, Ralph,' she said firmly. She smiled again.

'I do, Laura.'

I had spoken her name. I had heard myself saying it; I had felt the word in my mouth. I drew back, a coward once more.

It was getting late, I mumbled, and I had better go home. My mother was a worrier; she would be anxious by now.

She handed me my book and pecked at my cheek. 'You're forgiven. Visit me soon.'

I ran and walked, walked and ran, the way home.

In the sitting-room my mother and Mildred Harroway sat on either side of a table on which was a birthday cake with sixteen candles.

'I had it made for you, Ralphie. As a surprise.'

'I feel rather sick,' I said. 'I must lie on my bed.'

'He's been drinking. I noticed that expression more than once on my brother Charlie's face. And something strong, too, judging by the smell his breath's giving off.'

The following day I gave my courage a different name.

HERE

The window is spattered with rain and tiny dabs of blossom. I force myself to concentrate on the grey scene outside but tall Mildred insists that I return to this book: her face is still with me, her head with its dark hair-net that covers – and almost hides – her small bald patch, her fingers that drum relentlessly on the table. She tells me it is time I made the effort to understand her.

This woman is my bitterest enemy. She has no name for me: I am merely the son of my mother.

Since your visit yesterday [her letter begins, without formalities] your mother has been in a condition the like of which I have not seen her in for some years. She is as distressed as when your father died. You opened old scars. You may not have meant to but you did. Your mother feels things. It even hurt her when that woman your father nearly left her for passed away. I do not know why but there it is. As your mother's best friend I think I have some cause to write to you. You left her alone and now you return. You have no idea of the upsets that result. It takes all I have to make her herself again. I do not complain, it is my lot in life, I would rather be with your mother than any other person. We are happy as two sandpipers most of the time. I must get straight to the point. I am beating about the bush. I write this short message to ask you not to call on us again unless a case of emergency arises. Sickness or accident, God forbid. I ask you in all good faith. We are nearing the end, the two of us. It would be nice if whatever time is granted to us could be passed without hurts.

Have no fear. Your mother loves you. But it is me who cares for her. I am sorry about your wife. It would not be Christian of me to be otherwise. Of course I feel sorry for you. However we make our beds and we must lie on them.

M. HARROWAY

US

'United we stand,' Ellie whispered. 'Divided we fall.'

Mrs Chivers brought in the soup on a tray. 'Does your young man like consommé of beef, Elspeth?'

'I'll ask him. Do you like consommé of beef, Ralph?'

'I adore consommé of beef, yes.'

'Out of a tin, I suppose?' Mrs Chivers sent a pitying smile some inches above my head. 'This consommé of mine is the real thing, I'm proud to say. Strained through the sieve with my own hands.'

'Consommé is best', Major Chivers said, 'in the summer. Ice-cold. Like eating jelly. Most refreshing. Drop of sherry on the top and a slice of lemon.'

'It's more nourishing in the winter, Arnold.'

'Maybe so. But I prefer it when it looks like jelly.'

'Have you opened the wine yet?'

'Yes, dear.'

'We have wine with every meal, Mr Hicks. It's one of those luxuries we refuse to give up. And good wine, too—nothing too expensive but then nothing cheap either. Nothing from Spain or anywhere like that.'

'Or Australia.'

'My word, no, Arnold. Certainly not from Australia. Do you know, Elspeth, we went to the Shadbolts for dinner a few weeks back and not only did they serve Australian wine with the meal, they offered your father a glass of Cyprus sherry as an aperitif. They surely can't be feeling the pinch *that* badly.'

'Terrible plonk, it was. Tore at the gut.'

'And the Shadbolts, Mr Hicks—'

'Mummy, will you please call him Ralph?'

'Not until I know him better, Elspeth. I come from an age, dear, when it was considered impolite to be over-familiar on first acquaintance. You know my old-fashioned ways and how I stick to them. I was about to tell your young man about the Shadbolts. Well, Mr Hicks, they're a very good family—'

'Good, dear. Not *very* good. Not really top drawer. Money, though. They have money.'

'Yes, Arnold, you're right. I doubt whether their pedigree goes as far back as they care to maintain, but they do have a great deal of money. They live at The Grange, Mr Hicks. Have you seen it?'

'Not yet, Mrs Chivers.'

Major Chivers carved the roast lamb.

'It's a beautiful building. Wonderful architecture. A real piece of old England. What period is it, Arnold? Saxon?'

'Tudor. Tudor, dear. Saxon's earlier.'

Major Chivers splashed his shirt with mint sauce. He answered his wife's glare with a grin. 'Better put the blinds up, hadn't I, dear?' he said as he fixed his napkin tightly into his collar.

ME

Mummy's Ralphie wrote his name out. Ralph Hicks: the letters sloping right. Ralph Hicks: the letters sloping left. The letters now bold and upright, now bunched together. Ralph Hicks: there were hundreds of different ways of writing the two words that proclaimed his identity.

Mummy's Ralphie had a new signature every day. Unlike the other boys. They never changed: what they wrote said who they were.

COLD

'I'm not disturbing you, am I?'

'No, Mrs Dinsdale,' said Ellie. 'Come in.'

'I hate to inconvenience my clientele. I wouldn't normally call on you of an evening.' She placed herself delicately on the edge of a chair. 'But today is rather an exceptional day.'

Ellie asked her why it was.

'You've not heard the news?'

'What news?'

'About my mother? About Mrs Goacher?'

'No. What has happened?'

'She's dead, Mrs Hicks.' She raised her voice. 'She's dead, Mr Hicks.'

My rock had crumbled at last. My comfort. My source of warmth.

'How?'

'A tumour on her brain. In the street. Out shopping. The doctor who – who looked for the cause said she went like a light. Here one minute, gone the next.'

Ellie said how sorry we were.

'It was a sudden thing. The doctor who looked for the cause told me there was probably no pain. Everything went black, more than likely, and that was it. I shall miss her, for all her ways. She *was* my mother and there's a lot I have to thank her for.'

She refused the drink we offered. The nearest she had ever been to dipsomania was two cherry brandies one Christmas as a girl.

'I shall miss her around the house most. It will be less like a family concern now, Mother and Daughter seeing to the rooms and supervising. And she *was* a character, you have to agree.'

We agreed.

'She had her faults, but then who hasn't? No one's exempt. And she wasn't always as grateful to me as she ought to have been, though I say it myself. I'm sure she never expected in her wildest dreams to spend her old age in a house as pleasant as this, an apartment all to herself and me at hand to answer her every beck and call. But there you are. I mean, some children are quite heartless, the way they turf their old folks off into Homes – I can go to bed without *that* on my conscience, which is one blessing. Yes, my memories of her will be pleasant ones, in the main.'

Mad Mr Lavers would no longer cross himself. Tit would no longer be Ernest Dinsdale's downfall.

'I had my little cry at tea-time by myself in private. I feel all the better now for having let the tears out – the worst thing is to bottle it up, as they say. And I'm grateful for your sympathy, do believe me. I count it nothing short of a miracle, I honestly do, that she should have gone this morning, nice and fresh and clean. Being elderly, she wasn't always so particular about her person – as you may or may not have noticed – and I had to make a point of reminding her sometimes that the bathroom was in walking distance. But at eight this morning she had a good long soak in some of my essence and I put out a fresh change of undergarments for her, so the doctor who looked for the cause had no grounds for complaint on that score. That's what I like to think, anyway.'

She stood up. She smoothed her skirt down with both hands. She patted her hair.

'What on earth is he doing on your wall?'

Ellie explained. He was there to remind us.

'Forgive my saying, but I for one don't need reminding. The sight of that belly and those eyes! If I had nothing to look at but him, I'd soon have the miseries.'

HERE

They are with me now. My ghosts are assembled. I trust them to lead me somewhere.

But first I must see my cousin, Harry.

2

My mother knocked at the door.

'I've made you some nice coffee, Ralphie. Can I bring it in?'

'Yes.'

She placed the cup and saucer on the table, not too near my books in case of accidents, and not so far away from me that I couldn't drink without straining.

'I mustn't disturb your studies, must I?'

'My work's done.'

'Can I stay and sit with you?'

'Yes. If you want.'

'I have something to tell you. We can have a little talk. I'll pour a sherry and settle myself.'

Before we talked, would I mind turning off the wireless? It sounded like closet music. There was no such thing, I told her: it was chamber music. It was by Schubert. A closet was the same thing as a chamber, wasn't it? It was, at least, when she'd gone to school. Whatever it was, whoever wrote it, it set her nerves on edge.

In the street two boys played with a tennis ball. I watched them during the silence.

'I got a letter today. From your aunt.'

'Did you?'

'Your Aunt Kitty.'

'Who's she?'

'Oh now, you know your Aunt Kitty. You *do*. Your father's brother's wife who lives near Romford. Romford in Essex.'

'I don't remember.'

'You do. You're playing a game with me, Ralphie. I took you to see her and your Uncle Victor only a year or so ago.'

'*Her*.'

'There's a thing to say—*her*. She took a liking to you. She thought you a proper little gentleman.'

'Did she? Why?'

'Because you were polite.'

'Was I really, Mother? I didn't mean to be.'

What I'd meant to be was rude, bloodily and unforgivably, shattering the peace of small, neat Kitty and big, satisfied Victor, my father's elder brother who was still functioning, still making money; who was, despite his five years' advance in age, still living. I'd wanted to shake the foundations of their home, 'Restawhile'. I'd wanted to remind them of all I considered was alien to their lives, this smug pair in their vulgar comfort: uncomfortable matters like despair and loss. Especially loss—I missed my father. There had been nights when I'd grown almost demented at the thought of not seeing him again. I had even called on Miss Potter: she had seemed to me a more tangible reminder of his presence and his gentle ways. We had sat, the two of us, in her long room, discussing her plants. She had told me when they bloomed and how they grew.

But I'd answered my aunt's patronizing questions without a hint of sarcasm and had said nothing when Uncle Victor—leaning against the mantelpiece in a pose that was intended to suggest nonchalant authority—had embarked, without prompting, upon his political philosophy, a lengthy catalogue of fierce hates delivered with much benevolence.

The trouble with George Hicks, said Uncle Victor, was that once he had bought his newspaper shop he had been content. He had not progressed. A man should never pull his reins in until the very last minute.

My mother, to my horror, had nodded agreement.

'Read it for yourself.' She handed me Aunt Kitty's letter. It was written on scented notepaper headed 'Restawhile. Lights Lane.'

(I sit back and Auntie Kitty's immortal prose rushes into my

mind, every misplaced comma of it. I memorized her letter—
along with 'The Ancient Mariner' and 'Intimations of Immortality' and several Browning soliloquies: it would do for 'copy'
for a story I would publish in the school magazine, which I hoped
would find its way into 'Restawhile'. I wanted vengeance.)
She wrote:

My dear Mary.
It is a long time since I wrote I know but we have been
up to our ears in it as the saying goes. Victor has been made
a Councillor which pleases him of course and makes me very
proud. It is only what he deserves I should say after the work
he has put in over the years, There will be some changes
made if he has any say in the matter, He sends you and
your boy his kind regards.

She flowed on:

My real reason for writing is to ask a favour of you. Do you
remember our son, we christened him Harry. As you may
recall we had to have him put away when he was fifteen, he
is still in the same home which is in Kent, full address at
bottom of letter. Last week we received a letter from one of
the doctors, he said that Harry had improved, was taking
great strides to use his expression. We went to see him Victor
and myself and you would almost think he was like the rest
of us he was so nice and freindly.

From poetry to prose now:

This is all a roundabout way of asking you if you could see
your way to visiting him, this coming sunday for preference
as we shant be able to make it due to business of Victors, if
you and your boy could manage it we would be grateful as
we told Harry to expect visitors, and anyway it would make
a nice day in the country for you. Enclosed is £3 pounds to
cover cost of fare and meals. If we were free we would of
course take you in the car but a coach is the next best thing,

I would recommend it over a train because you can enjoy the view more, I must end now if I am to catch the post in time, I will phone you on monday to find out how it all went. That is if you go but I am sure you will,

Yours Affec, KITTY.

Kitty was sure; Kitty was right. The following Sunday a coach took us to the asylum in Kent.

My mother wore a violet suit and a violet hat trimmed with pink chiffon. She considered this her best outfit. Despite it being August, and extremely hot, she also took her fur wrap, which reeked of moth-balls. Her face was powdered a light pink and her cheeks were highlighted with rouge.

She insisted, before we left the house that morning, that I wore a tie. I was to show some respect; in the course of the day I would be meeting important people like doctors, who would be offended by slovenliness. And I was to wear my weddings and funerals suit that old Mr Marks had made up for me out of that lovely piece of left-over cloth. She knew it was on the heavy side, but I owed it to the poor boy we were going to visit to look my smartest. I was young enough to be susceptible to blackmail: she threatened tears (so rare now as to be a frightening prospect) if I didn't slick my hair down with brilliantine.

'I've put cologne on your hanky. If you sweat, dab your face.'

On the coach, on the endless journey there, I imagined myself far away, in company more sophisticated and congenial than that I was burdened with. I could have borne the journey with Miss Potter, enjoyed it even, felt pride.

The book on my lap was my only protection:

The worlds whole sap is sunke:
The generall balme th'hydroptique earth hath drunk,
Whither, as to the beds-feet, life is shrunke,
Dead and enterr'd; yet all these seem to laugh,
Compar'd with mee, who am their Epitaph.

How soothing I found those harsh images as my mother chattered about the fine weather and the beauties of Kent we would shortly be seeing. They helped me forget the gaudiness of her dress, the frequent clicking of her new false teeth and the strong smell of peppermint on her breath.

We arrived. We gaped.

'They have nice grounds here. Those roses. Oh, and look: dahlias. It's a very old-fashioned building, isn't it?'

'Victorian.'

'Was that when it was?'

'Yes.'

'It's very big. All the people that are here! You wouldn't reckon there would be so many come to visit at a place like this.'

'No.'

'I wonder if they're all relations.'

'I wonder.'

'Visiting starts at three. What does your watch say?'

'Five to three.'

'Five minutes to go then. Do you see the fountain?'

'Yes. Yes.'

'Shall we walk round the lawn once more?'

'Yes, Mother.'

'That woman, Ralphie, looks like royalty the way she's got up.'

'George the Third was mad.'

'Was he?'

'Yes.'

'Look, Ralphie, they're going in. I wonder what he's like. Years ago he looked like any other boy.'

'Like me?'

'His hair was different. His was blond. And his eyes, if I recall, were big. Yours are smaller than his were.'

'Are.'

'Are, then. But he must have changed.'

'Not his eyes.'

'Not them, I don't suppose.'

My mother asked a nurse to direct us to Mr Harry Hicks.

'Oh yes. He's been with us a long time. One of our regulars.' She laughed. 'The Men's Wing's this way.'

We walked behind the nurse, who led us along several corridors. My mother said loudly, 'Harry Hicks is my nephew.'

'Is he really?'

'My son's cousin.'

'Is he?'

Our voices, our footsteps echoed. The nurse's keys, dangling from a piece of string tied round her waist, clinked as she walked. She stopped to open a door with one of them.

'I have to lock all the doors behind me. As a precaution.'

'Oh? Are they dangerous?'

'The dangerous boys and girls are kept in a special wing. Visitors aren't allowed there. The patients' rooms have padded walls.'

'Like I saw in a film once.'

'Really?'

We stopped at another door, which the nurse opened with another key. My mother, attempting a smile, said 'You'd think you were in a prison.'

'I hope not.'

'I didn't mean—'

'Great personal care is taken of every patient we have here.'

'I'm sure it is. I'm sure of that.'

'Your Mr Hicks has a most pleasant room, with a view of the gardens.'

'That's nice for him.'

We walked on.

The nurse said 'You don't say much, do you, young man?'

'No.'

'It's his being in a strange place,' my mother explained.

'The age you are, you can't be shy.'

'I am, though.'

'I bet you're not shy with your girl friend.'

'He's too busy with his studies to bother with a girl friend. Aren't you, Ralphie?'

'He wouldn't tell you. Boys never tell their mothers about their girl friends. Do they?'

'No,' I agreed.

'What's your young lady's name?'

'Estella.'

'That's unusual. It's gipsy sounding. What's her other name?'

'She doesn't have one. She's adopted. She lives with a Miss Havisham.'

'You're leading me on, young man. You can't adopt if you're a Miss. You have to be a Mrs. And have a Mr in the house.'

As she opened the last door she said 'He's got a sense of humour, your son.'

'Oh—yes. He has.'

She locked the door behind us.

'Here we are. I'll take you in.'

Harry was very fat and very white. His blond hair was cropped short. He had no eyebrows.

'Here are two nice people to see you.'

My mother stepped forward. 'We've come to see you, Harry. You remember me—your aunt?'

He stared at each of us in turn. He asked the nurse how she knew we were nice.

'I've had a long chat with them.'

Harry rose from his chair.

'Your trouser buttons, Harry Hicks. Do them up. And turn your back on us as you do so.'

Harry grinned. There were gaps between his chipped teeth. He walked to the window. The nurse followed him. We heard her say 'Boys who do that go blind.' Then, in a louder, jollier voice, she said 'This young man who's come to visit has a sense of humour.'

Harry, still grinning, looked at me. 'Are you crafty?' he asked.

'I don't know.'

'Yes, you do. I'm crafty. I know I'm crafty. I can see myself when I'm being crafty.'

'Harry Hicks, you're usually well-behaved.'

'I'm not. I put a knife in my father's leg.'

'Did you?' I asked him, intrigued.

'While he was sleeping. Then he woke. There was blood ... My father came to see me. He said he was my father. I couldn't tell. But he said he was. I couldn't put a knife in him because I hadn't got one. I eat with a spoon.'

'Harry Hicks, you're not to be morbid.'

'No. The sun's out.'

'Isn't it a lovely day?' said my mother brightly.

'Who are you?'

'I'm your Aunt Mary.'

'And who's he?'

'Tell him who you are, Ralphie.'

'My name's Ralph.'

'My name's Harry. An H and an A and an R and an R and a Y.'

'I'll leave you with your nice relations, Harry Hicks. You must have a lot to say to one another.'

'I've nothing to say.'

'Yes, you have.'

'Nothing to anyone.'

'He knows I won't be cross with him. That's why he's being naughty.' She added, winking at me, 'I shall be outside.' She left.

We stood in silence.

My mother said 'I think I'll sit down, Harry. Ralph and me have been on our feet for quite some while.'

Harry bowed, indicating the chair with his right hand.

'Do sit down. Do sit down.'

My mother sat.

We listened to the electric mower as it trimmed the lawn.

'Speak,' Harry said. 'Speak if you want to.'

'We brought you—didn't we, Ralphie?—a little present.'

'Present? What present?'

'Some chocolates.'

'Eat them.'

'Don't you like chocolates?'

'I do not require them. They are of no use to me. Do you speak to each other?'

'I beg your—'

'You two. Do you exchange words?'

'Of course we do.'

'I thought you did.'

My mother, embarrassed, returned to her favourite topic. 'What a lovely day it is.'

'Today's one of my bad days.'

'Why is it, Harry?'

'I don't answer questions.'

He asked me if I had ever stabbed my father

'No.'

'Why not?'

'I never wanted to.'

'I see. Shall we stare at each other? I can stare you out. I am thirty years old.'

'Are you?'

'I told you, didn't I? I said. Ten plus ten plus ten. There are stars when it's dark.'

'Yes. You're right. There are,' said my mother.

'I prefer the night.'

'Why's that?'

'I prefer it. Do you prefer it, what's-your-name?'

'Yes. Ralph.'

'The Milky Way.'

'Yes.'

'Clusters.' He lifted his arms above his head. 'Constellations.'

'Yes.'

'Shining.'

I asked him if he had a telescope. Lowering his arms, he said 'No. I look straight at them. I look at them and cry. I like to cry. I can cry for days. Shall I cry for you?'

'No, Harry. Thank you. Not just now.'

'Then eat your chocolates, Aunt.'

She smiled and nodded. She sighed.

'Well ...'

'Well well well well –'

'It *has* been a nice visit, Harry. Would you like us to come again?'

'I don't care.'

'We will, then.'

'You will. You will.'

'Goodbye, Harry.'

'I have a dog inside me. He's quiet all day. He howls at night.'

'Goodbye, Harry.'

'Bye bye. Bye bye.'

Wasn't it terrible, wasn't it sad? A man of thirty to be so like a child. To be so horribly white and fat. Of course it wasn't the kind of fat you got from eating too much, it was glandular. We should thank the good Lord we'd been blessed with glands that were normal.

And to say he had a dog inside him! Only a person who was really mad would talk in that way. 'I have a dog inside me,' he'd said. The poor, poor creature. He was a thing. He wasn't a man. He hadn't a life.

Her eyes glowed. Her nose twitched.

We were home. The sane world was about us. We stood together in the shop and looked around: everything was in place – the brass till, newly polished; the jars of sweets and the little hammer for breaking toffee; the pile of newspapers, neatly bound with string, which Mildred Harroway had been unable to sell for us that morning.

We went into the kitchen.

'The kettle's on for cocoa, Ralphie. There's cheese in the larder if you want something to eat.'

'All right.'

'My mouth feels awful. I don't like having these new teeth in all day. I wonder, honestly, if I'll ever get used to them. I suppose I will; Mr Cottie said I will. He said they were the best he could do for me. Would you mind, Ralphie, if I took them out? Could you bear to look at me?'

'Yes.'

'You're sure?'

'Yes, Mother.'

'You won't pull a face?'

'No, Mother.'

'I hate to be seen when I'm not my best. Even by you, my own son.' She crossed the passage and went into the bathroom. She returned soon after. 'Now who's a glamour-puss then?'

'Yes,' I said, without looking.

'I can put them back in, I'll look less ugly, but the pain—'

'Shut up, Mother.' I banged my fist on the kitchen table.

'All I said was—'

'I heard you. You talk and talk. You never leave me alone. You never say anything. That lunatic makes more sense.'

'He's not really a—'

'Yes, he is. He's bloody crazy. You said yourself he was, as soon as we left that place. He's bloody mad and you know it, and with that woman, that Kitty, for a mother I can't say I blame him.'

She said, very quietly, 'It was his father he went for.'

'What?'

'He went for his father. With the knife.'

'Well, I don't blame him for that either.'

'Shall I turn the wireless on, Ralphie? Some nice music might cheer us up. We need cheering, really, after seeing Harry.'

'Do what you want.'

'There.' She listened for a moment. 'I'll prepare our cocoa. A nightcap will do us both good; we'll sleep all the better. That's an old song they're playing. I was singing that when I was ever so young. Not that I had a voice, so to speak, not a proper singing voice, but I did like to open my throat a bit when I was young, before George, before your father that is, came along and swept me off my feet.'

'Did you, Mother?'

'Oh, I did. There's the kettle whistling.'

'Yes, Mother. There's the kettle whistling.'

'Time for cocoa, then.'

'Yes, Mother.'

She hummed a phrase of the music.

'You must write and thank your aunt for our little trip. You write a nice letter. When you *do* write, I wouldn't mention, if I were you, what he said about his father. Victor wouldn't want to read that. Nor about his buttons. His trouser buttons, Ralphie, being open — nor about them. Is your drink hot enough?'

'Yes.'

'Why don't you eat some cheese, Ralphie? It's Mr Horsman's best Cheddar.'

'I'm not hungry.'

'You should be, after such a day. You ought to be able to swallow a horse between two mattresses, as Charlie Harroway says when he sees so much as a biscuit. Do eat some, Ralphie, for *my* sake. It *is* English, after all, not foreign.'

'Right, Mother, I'll eat some. If you will only stop.'

'Am I talking a lot? I'm sure I do talk a lot sometimes. That *is* my way. I do get so lonely, even with you with me. You *are* all I have; all that's left. Your father and me, those last years, we had our words, you heard us, he complained of my little mind, he told me so often about that woman and how she understood him, what sympathy he got — even so, Ralphie, though we had words, now he's gone for ever ...' She sniffed loudly. 'I hope I don't sound sorry for myself. I certainly hope I don't sound that.'

I looked at my mother and began to cry. I laid my head on the kitchen table. The oilcloth cooled my cheek.

'I wouldn't be jealous of any girl you've got.'

'Girl?'

'The one you mentioned, Ralphie. Gipsy sounding.'

'She's in a book. Estella. She doesn't exist.'

'Oh? I should have known. I *am* ignorant about books and such. You'll be clever, Ralphie – cleverer even than your father was, with your education, with the chances ahead of you. You'll prosper. Prosper *is* the word, isn't it?'

'Yes.'

'You asked me to stop, didn't you? I will, don't worry. I keep talking and I look so frightful. Don't cry, Ralphie. Men shouldn't. You're grown now.'

'It was seeing him.'

'I know it was.'

'Nothing makes sense to me in this bloody world.'

'It will.'

'He spelt his name out.'

'He did, too.'

I looked up at her. She covered her mouth with a hand.

'An R and an A and an L and a P and an H.'

'Spells Ralph, Ralphie.'

Then we laughed.

I despair of ever knowing why I cried that evening. I want to think I shed tears of pity for my mother but I cannot persuade myself that this was so.

Perhaps it was Harry I felt for. Perhaps I imagined myself with cropped hair taking comfort from stars, spooning food into my slack mouth, laughing at the nurses who locked me in at nights.

Yet I am amazed now, whatever the reason, that I cried so freely, that we laughed together so happily afterwards.

Hours later, though, a shower of pebbles woke me.

3

ME–US

The café I sat in had brown wallpaper and a stale smell. There was a photograph of King George VI, in naval uniform, above the service-hatch. Outside, the rain fell steadily.

Miss Elspeth Chivers, teacher of Arts and Crafts – employed, like me, at dank St Clement's – entered and removed her raincoat, which she shook gently. She hung it on a stand near the door.

'May I sit with you, Mr Hicks?'

'Yes.'

'Am I disturbing your reading?'

'No.'

She sat, staring straight at me. I smiled. She continued to stare. I smiled again and asked her if she required tea (red water) or coffee (brown water). I repeated the question in a louder voice.

'Yes. Thank you.'

'Which?'

'Tea. Please.'

We drank in silence for a while. Then, for five minutes or so, we agreed that the weather was terrible. After which she inquired if I had had a good day at the school. I replied that it had been much like any other.

Suddenly she began to talk about herself, her eyes demanding my complete attention. She wanted to be of some real use in the world, to show the poor children she taught at St Clement's that there were things to value despite their homes, despite the

81

indifference and neglect they were all too familiar with. She found it inspiring work. Because—I must understand—her way of life up till now had been totally different; useless, really—what she meant was, it depressed her into the ground just to think about it.

Nevertheless, she described her childhood. And her youth, and her adolescence. A major's daughter, she'd been brought up in India in an atmosphere of fêtes and gymkhanas and teas with the officers' wives. Could I picture it: the croquet matches, the beggars dying in the streets? Yes, I said, I could, clearly. Back in England, Major and Mrs and little Elspeth—what a bloody name, Elspeth—had settled in Bournemouth, in a house like many others, without servants. There, for fifteen years, her Mummy and Daddy had played out a parody of their former life: managing, on Daddy's army pension and his income from the bank (where he worked in a distinctly menial capacity), to hold occasional bridge evenings and one small cocktail party each month. Daddy, a major in name only, had become a genial buffer, seldom roused to any strong emotion—even indecent anger against the coloured invasion, hitherto his favourite subject. ('I know the Coloured Mind. I've spent my life keeping it in check.') His geniality appalled her more. And Mummy—well, poor Mummy had found there was nothing to occupy her: no servant problems and very few people to put in their place—she enjoyed (and you couldn't really practise it with any grace in Bournemouth) letting certain persons know, lest they forget in future, how to behave at table, what words not to use, what clothes not to wear, what drinks—even—not to drink. She had also enjoyed, with an enthusiasm approaching ferocity, her Good Works days: they had come round all too rarely, but when they had she had donned her picture hat and an especially bright smile that only she knew how to quickly transform into an unnerving glare. Mummy with a tin in her hand was an awesome sight.

Then, after informing me that they now lived in the country—the squire and his lady in miniature—she apologized for boring me with her family saga.

'It's your turn now,' she said with a smile.

To my surprise I mentioned my father – and my mother – **and** the shop in Camberwell.

'Was it a poor district?'

'Part of it.'

'Were your neighbours poor?'

'Some of them.'

'Your father obviously wasn't, since he owned a shop.'

'It was a small shop. It was poky.'

It was time, I thought, to return to the weather again. Or to cough and get up and say I was sorry, I had an appointment, this friend of mine hated to be kept waiting, and the rain was –

'You aren't such a mystery.'

'Me?'

'You. Mr Ralph Hicks. You aren't so aloof after all.'

She told me then that she had been too frightened to speak to me before. It had been a question of taking the plunge. Anyway, the plunge had been taken – she had chattered, hadn't she, like a parrot? – and I *was* human, she hadn't ever doubted it; what she meant was, I looked so forbidding, so contained in myself, and she *had* been warned, although she shouldn't say, that I was a very distant kind of person ... Why didn't we go and have dinner together?

So we went.

AFTER

A new room in a new house in a new street in a new part of London. Old roses on the walls, pink ones, but faded to brown nearer the window: the sun has mellowed them. And a green carpet which is also yellow. The shade which covers the bulb which dangles from the centre of the white and grey ceiling turns everything blue at night.

I have come here because of the state of Mrs Dinsdale's bathroom.

'I was awfully bloody unfair to them, wasn't I?'

'To whom, Elspeth?'

'My parents. This afternoon. When I told you about them. I made them sound like caricatures, didn't I? Monsters. Would you have guessed from the way I spoke that I really love them?'

'Yes.'

'Be honest with me, please. What I mean is, Ralph, is that it turns my heart over, the way they behave.'

As I kicked the quilt from the bed I wondered if I was mad as well as drunk. Why should I involve myself with Miss Elspeth Chivers? She wasn't even a beauty: her breasts and hips were large.

'Don't cry any more,' I said, and my gentleness surprised me.

We were cold. We huddled together.

Later on, she laughed. 'It isn't only the drink, is it?' she asked softly. 'I seem to have a virgin on top of me.'

'You have.'

Another surprise for me: my honest reply. And my pride in making it.

'My lamb,' she said. 'My Ralph.'

She guided me in.

There was sunshine, fittingly, the next morning. She lay sleeping. I left the bed.

Perhaps, I thought as I stood by the window, I shall grow into love.

I went into the kitchen.

Love, I hoped, would brighten my world. It wanted brightening.

I brewed coffee and took it to her. We kissed. I accepted her breasts as they were offered.

I entered without assistance.

We arrived at St Clement's with our arms linked.

AFTER

The world reduced to old roses under a blue light. That was my province. That was where I functioned.

I thought of them: my father, my mother, tall Mildred, cropped Harry, Ellie – for a time *my* Ellie – the Major and Mrs, and my grandmother – her toothless Albert laid out, the soap and the water to make him sweet.

And Bernard, the teachers, the children, the boy who smiled. The others, the countless others: the hands shaken, the looks shared. The lives I had turned away from by choice and the lives I would never enter.

For all my education – Mummy's Ralphie thriving and growing; for all those books – I had felt no stirrings at the prospect of entering another's life, of being radiantly submerged.

Except when my father had gone, when it was no longer possible, when there were only pebbles to answer me – showers of them, each dark night. And with Ellie, who was now ash, who had awakened me once to the possibilities I would continue to keep out of my reach.

US

Mildred Harroway opened the door. She saw Ellie first and muttered 'Who – ?' Then she noticed me.

'Oh, it's you. You had better come in. Your mother *is* at home.'

'I'm sorry to call like this,' I immediately apologized. 'But it's difficult to make arrangements to come over now that you no longer have a phone.'

'There is such a thing as the post.'

'We decided to come on the spur of the moment,' Ellie said. 'It was a sudden idea.'

'We might have been out. It's fine today and we might have

gone down to the gardens to sit in the sun. As chance would have it, we didn't. You are lucky to find us both in.'

My mother called out, 'Who is it, Milly?'

'Your son, Mary. And some young woman.' She looked at Ellie. 'I didn't catch your name.'

I again apologized. 'Let me introduce you. Miss Elspeth Chivers, Miss Mildred Harroway.'

'Pleased to meet you, I'm sure. Had you both planned to stay a while?'

We both replied 'Well, we —'

'Because if you had, then I suggest you leave your coats out here. The heating's on and you won't feel the benefit when you do actually leave.'

'You have central heating?' Ellie asked.

'Every modern convenience, yes.' She added, as we turned a corner of the hall, 'Except the telephone. We decided against having one because we have few real friends. Those we *do* have live hereabouts. There wasn't any need.'

Ellie said, very gently, that she understood.

My mother rose as we entered. She clutched the table to steady herself. I went to her and kissed the cheek she offered me.

'We weren't expecting you, Ralphie. We might have been out. You didn't write.'

I made my third apology as she smiled and nodded to Ellie. 'How do you do?'

Ellie came forward. 'How do you do, Mrs Hicks?'

'Mother, this is Elspeth Chivers. Elspeth, my mother.'

'Ralphie didn't write to say he was bringing you to visit. I'm certain I don't look my best, I know I don't feel it —'

'You look very good, Mrs Hicks.'

'It's nice of you to say, but I wish you'd given me notice, Ralphie, as it were, to prepare myself. I feel I look an old fright even if I don't.'

'You don't.'

'Well, it's nice of you, as I say.'

'Why doesn't everyone sit down? There *are* chairs about —

we're not in a field.'

Mildred plumped the cushions on the sofa. 'Down you go again, Mary. When your back is hurting you, the sensible thing is to rest it. You've been standing long enough.'

'Yes, Milly. Thank you. I was only being polite.'

'Please sit down, Mrs Hicks.'

'Yes, yes.' Mildred held my mother's elbow as she lowered herself. 'I doubt if I'd last if it wasn't for Milly. She's better than any nurse to me; she sees I'm kept in trim better than any doctor.'

'We have to be careful at our age, whether we like it or not. I suppose I had best make some tea for your guests.'

'Yes please, Milly.'

Ellie wondered if she could help.

'Not really, no, thank you.'

'The kitchen is Milly's concern and hers alone. All trespassers are prosecuted.' She laughed. The trace of a smile formed on Mildred's lips and vanished. 'I usually bake a cake for visitors. But we've only biscuits, I'm afraid, as we weren't expecting anyone.'

'Please don't go to any trouble.'

'It's no trouble. Putting a few biscuits on a plate is no trouble.'

'Let's have Garibaldis, Milly. Ralphie likes those.'

Mildred said 'Very well' and left the room. My mother smiled at Ellie, who smiled back. She nodded. 'George, my husband that is, Ralphie's father, called them "fly cemeteries", Garibaldis.'

'Did he?'

'That was his name for them, yes. I always told him it was morbid of him and he always laughed.'

I asked her if she was feeling healthy, apart from her back.

'I won't say I'm fighting fit. You know me, I never have been. No, I don't think there's anything wrong with me.'

'That's good,' said Ellie.

'You must excuse me, I'm in a state, Ralphie calling so un-expected, your name has gone out of my head.'

'Elspeth Chivers. It's an awful name, isn't it, Elspeth? Ralph calls me Ellie.'

'Oh, I don't agree it's awful. "Elspeth" sounds nice to my ears. I can think of a dozen worse things I wouldn't like to be called. Ralphie calls you Ellie?'

'Yes. Yes, he does, Mrs Hicks.'

'Ellie? Yes, I see.'

'Yes.'

'I don't want to sound prying, I certainly hope I don't sound that, but I'd like to ask you if you work for your living?'

'I do indeed, Mrs Hicks. My job is the same as Ralph's. I teach at his school.'

'You do, do you?' She stared at Ellie. 'What do you teach?'

'Painting, Mrs Hicks. Drawing.'

'Do you?' She went on staring. Minutes passed before she said, 'My son there, Ralphie, was brilliant at school.'

'Now, Mother—'

'You were. It can't be denied, it's something you can't argue with, all the teachers said. He *was*, Miss— Miss—'

'Chivers, Mother.'

'Ellie, Mrs Hicks, please. I'm Ellie.'

'Well, Miss Ellie, I mean Ellie, he was. French, history, books— some of them his father had read, I couldn't, they were beyond me, though I won't say I'm stupid, words and things I was never able to grasp—books, I swear, that no one had looked at for years or more. I took such pride in him. Anything he put his mind to he got the hang of. You *did*, Ralphie. I don't care how many faces you pull.'

'Ralph's clever, Mrs Hicks.'

'Oh, he is. He was. He was so clever, he had everything before him. He could have gone so far. He came to a stop, though. Didn't you, Ralphie? Just like that. He never told me the reason. I asked him Lord knows how many times what his plans were, what he was going to do with his future, and could I get a sensible reply out of him? I could not. I told him he didn't make sense to me, I even begged with him for his father's sake—'

'Mother—'

'Yes. I must stop, mustn't I? Once I get started, my mind goes back, I find myself worrying and I shouldn't, my health ... ' Her voice trailed away. She smiled brightly at Ellie. 'Milly makes good tea. She's a great improvement on me in the kitchen. There are days when I can't even boil so much as an egg. Ralphie will tell you, I'm sure he has already, how I panic sometimes.'

'I haven't, Mother.'

'He hasn't, Mrs Hicks.'

'It's true, anyhow. I shouldn't talk against myself, should I? Milly snaps my head off when she catches me doing it.'

'Does she?'

'Oh yes, oh yes.' She continued, in a whisper: 'She says it's the one thing I should never do, it gives people leeway.'

'She's right, Mrs Hicks.'

'You think so?'

'Yes.'

'Milly *is* right about most things.'

We were silent until Mildred appeared. 'Are you Mary's son's girl friend?' she asked Ellie.

'Yes, she is —'

'Yes, I am. We love each other. We plan to marry.'

AFTER

Before, there had been nothing wrong. The room had been so large and so much light had streamed in.

Faces stared at me from the walls: the hungry child, the impassive woman. I closed my eyes and the red fog returned.

US

'The word has gone right out of my mind,' said Mrs Chivers. 'It's most annoying. It was used to describe artists starving in garrets.'

'Bohemian,' I suggested.

'Yes. Yes, I think that's the word that best describes this place.'

'Are you intending a compliment, Mummy, or the reverse?'

'Well, dear, in all truth, it isn't as bad as I was expecting. I mean no offence to Ralph'—she swallowed on my name—'but I was rather dreading coming here today. I know what a rare capacity you have for martyrdom and I seriously thought you'd deposited yourself in some slum. Did you put wine vinegar in this vinaigrette?'

'Yes.'

'It tastes just a little too sharp, that's why I asked. No, there's nothing wrong with this room that some fresh paint and a few decent pieces wouldn't put right. If you *have* to be so modern, if you *must* insist on living together before marriage, I suppose here is as good as anywhere else to stay. It's all right as a stop-gap.'

'It's no stop-gap, Mummy. We intend living here after we're married. Don't we, Ralph?'

'Yes, Ellie. We do.'

'Surely not, Elspeth'—I stood corrected, Ellie's name was most definitely Elspeth—'surely not. Not in this room. It's large, I grant you, but it's still a room. It isn't a flat.'

'It appeals to us. The light. The view.'

'What view? Roof-tops, pigeons, chimneys? Television aerials? They don't constitute any view *I* could bear to look at for long.'

'You won't be living with us, Mummy. Think of me for once; of what I want. I want Ralph. He doesn't have a rosy complexion and he doesn't come from your mythical good family. His bloody blood isn't of the bluest. I want him and I want to live here with him in this room—that is what I want. Can you hear? Oh, Mummy, why can't you open yourself to me? There's nothing and no one in your way. Why, please, can't you?'

'That avocado was very nice. It could have been riper but I enjoyed it, even so. Can I help you in any way with the next course?'

Ellie got up and gathered the dishes together without replying.

We looked into our wine as she went into the kitchen.

'Do you think she *can* manage?'

'Yes.'

'I *did* offer.'

AFTER

I saw her face. Ants came out of her eyes.

US

I was near to happiness at last, talking about myself. I ran it through, even from my boyish days. I was only mildly drunk: there would be no mention of Miss Potter or my father's love for her or the showers of pebbles. Nothing but Mummy's Ralphie breaking loose.

And I did break loose. How I thrived and grew; how ambitious I had been to win every prize, to receive the startled praises of boys and masters: I talked and talked. I was the brightest star in Camberwell's intellectual firmament. She listened, as no one had done before. I had given no one else the opportunity.

We were cold. We huddled together.

AFTER

'Ralph,' Mrs Chivers said, not obviously swallowing, 'you must come down to the cottage one day. One week-end. As soon as the summer shows itself. Or earlier, if you wish.'

'Yes.' The Major lifted my hand and shook it. 'Yes, you must. Fresh air. Long walks. Decent food. What you need.'

'You are not to blame yourself. He's not to—is he, Arnold?'

'No. Not to blame. Most certainly not.'

'Is that clear to you? You are not to blame. I only wish some-body was – it would give me a dreadful kind of comfort at the very least. I failed to teach her a sense of proportion. Butchering herself – ' She shuddered, drawing her astrakhan coat tightly about her. Then she cleared her throat, as if to cleanse it of the two words she had amazed herself by uttering. She started again:

'Doing what she did was entirely in character. I take no pride in telling you that.'

I watched them until they reached the gate. The Major turned and sent me a wave that ended, ridiculously, in a salute. The army had protected him from life and its protocol protected him now: it was his one certainty, his one sure thing. His gesture signalled defiance and survival for all its absurdity.

US

Lizards slithered over stones. We walked, arms linked, with the smells of orange and lemon.

Then, after the heat, the absolute coldness of the church, the soothing dark. The gradual emergence of mosaics and tombs.

Outside, we sat on the steps, drinking a green liqueur that the monks had brewed. Beyond cypresses, the city lay below us, delicately tinted.

I prayed that Ellie wouldn't speak – 'We're in Paradise, aren't we, Ralph?', 'Who would have thought, a month ago, we'd be sitting here?' – and my prayer was answered.

On the way to the fort, she put her arm through mine. When we arrived, the city still below, a wedding group was there: photos being taken, wine being drunk. A vast happy family grinned at us. A week before, my mother had missed the white: the lack of ceremony had made her cry. Perhaps, like some others, we would one day have a proper service, with a vicar, with all the words – it would, as it were, clinch the matter, wouldn't it?

AFTER

It was clear to all these people that she had been sick with love of me. I scratched my chin, it was something to do, while they stared. The balance of her mind had been disturbed.

The coroner warmed his hands on a dusty radiator. The clusters of blond hairs that hung from his nostrils were something to look at.

'She knew what she was doing, Mr Hicks.'

'Yes?'

'She severed the main arteries.'

'Yes?'

'Usually it's the wrists.'

He patted my shoulder. He was sorry, this was a tragic case, one wondered about one's fellow creatures as one sat in the court.

US

New curtains, a new tea-pot (the spout on mine had been kept in place with sticking-plaster), a Spanish rug, a bedspread: Ralph's room underwent its transformation. It was Ellie's and Ralph's now, the happy pair's. It was a love-nest, a palace.

'You could show a little more enthusiasm,' she said.

'What for?'

'What for? Oh, Ralph, for what I've done.' She continued in mock-Cockney: 'For working me poor fingers to the bone.'

'Yes,' I said. 'Yes.'

'What do you mean – yes?'

'What I mean is –' I looked at her, my eyes opened wide. She hesitated before laughing. 'I mean, it looks very –' what did it look? '– comfortable.'

And it did. Everything shone: the windows, the desk, and the brass posts at the foot of my father's bed. Especially those.

'Where *did* you buy that lovely bed, Ralph? I intended to ask

you the morning after the night of the consummation but somehow I forgot.' She giggled.

'It was my father's.'

'Your father's, Ralph? Why not your father's and mother's?'

'Because it wasn't.'

'They didn't share it?'

'I can't remember them doing so.'

It seemed, one night, that I would never leave the beach. The
sea withdrew; the sky changed to pebble. I awoke screaming.
I removed my pyjamas, which were damp with sweat. I went out
to the hall to see what time it was. Oh God, only two—four long
hours until morning. Without thinking, I opened the door of the
spare room, the room we always tidied when relatives or friends
of the family came to stay: old boxes of bills and letters to sort
through; odd chairs to artfully position above the holes in the
carpet. The objects assembled there had found a last resting-place
before the ignominy of the rag-and-bone man's cart: my father's
bed was the newest addition. I lifted the blanket and touched the
mattress. I listened as a tom-cat wailed. He was the property of
Mr Dacre, the chimney-sweep next door; one of his ears had
been bitten off and he was said to have fathered more kittens than
any other cat in Camberwell. I lay down, already drowsy. I got
up again and turned The Monarch of the Glen to the wall.
Beneath the blanket once more I fell asleep.

'I asked you a question, Ralph.'

'Did you? What was it?'

'I said something to the effect that wasn't it odd, working
people—what I mean is, a working-class couple—sleeping in
separate beds?'

'Yes. Very odd.'

'Why did they?'

'There was no love left, I suppose.'

'Why wasn't there? You must know.'

'I don't.'

Laura Potter. She was younger. Her teeth were whiter and her
hair was red.

'I don't, Ellie.'
'Are you sure?'
'Yes. Do I lie to you?'
'I hope not. No, Ralph, of course not.'
She kissed me.

AFTER

My dear Ralph,

Apologies are in order. When I rang yesterday I called you a cunt and a fucking cold fish. My phraseology was as choice as it was inexact. But easily the most unforgivable thing I did was to say I hoped you would rot in hell – really, how monstrous of me. Why is it that practising atheists so often resort to the same vulgar methods as His Lot? What *am* I going on about? – I must bring myself instantly to heel and let you know without any more delay that I'm truly sorry for my melodramatic lapse of Thursday April 3rd at 5 p.m. precisely. Please forgive me.

I offer one excuse. It must have been obvious from my slurred speech that I had been at the bottle. I had. I must have consumed more gin yesterday than ever Mesdames Gamp and Prig managed to knock back in all their jolly sessions over the tea-table. By evening I was so pissed that I had to forgo taking Culture to the Underprivileged – the first (and I sincerely hope, the last) time I have missed a class. Fortunately I passed out round about nine (I spent the night on the kitchen floor) just as I was feeling in the mood for a little lavatory-prowling. The last occasion I did that in an inebriated condition was when Mums died and I think I told you what the consequences were: an appearance in court and a heavy fine. The magistrate called me a shameful man and so did a certain Sunday newspaper.

Shameful or not, I had a good long sleep. It was while I was coming to life again this morning with the aid of cold water that I remembered ringing you up and insulting you. Ralph, take my word for it that you are not a cunt. I was so shaken by Ellie's death I had to call somebody something and you, I'm afraid, were the best target. No one – not even me, the first of the stone-casters – could have prevented the silly bitch from taking her life: that's a fact I am all too horribly sure of.

Oh dear, she was often so impossible, with her message of Universal Love and how the world would be a happier place if we were all nice to each other and Communism *could* work if we all made the effort – yes, yes, yes. Poor simple girl, so guilty about the luxury she had been brought up in. There was many a time, Ralph, when I came dangerously near to hitting her – that bloody pitying look that came over her face; that talk about my 'condition': she wanted so much to help everyone. It must have finally dawned on her that she couldn't, but that's only my theory.

She loved you of course (Make way for another theory!) but I think she loved her idea of you more. The longer she lived with you, the farther away you seemed to get from her – she told me. You were on her mind ages before she ever spoke to you, she'd seen you at the school and she'd fallen. It was that haggard face of yours (no rudeness intended) I suppose, that Pale And Interesting air you give off. Those unplumbed depths. From her first glimpse of you you were a marked man.

This was supposed to be a short note of apology, and it's ended up like a bloody volume of memoirs. One more thing – I shan't be at the funeral, whenever it is. All that hateful ritual. I will see you as soon as our lives have returned to their stable, dull old jog-trots.

Once again, forgive me for my telephonic bid to the title

of Uncrowned Queen of the Heavy Breathers. At my age I should have known better.

Love, B.

US

We had left our love-nest for a week-end in the country. All Sunday morning we climbed stiles, ran across fields, hid from each other behind trees or hedges. Dew turned my brown shoes black.

Lunch was taken on the lawn.

Ellie and the Major and Mrs lay in deck-chairs and slept. I wandered off: blue above and green below; no voices, no involvement.

But I *was* involved. The sullen teacher whom the children feared had brightened lately, had been seen with his arm around Miss Chivers, who was so warm and kind, whose lessons no one ever played truant from — What a surprise, to walk in one day and discover that Mr Hicks was almost human!

Almost human Mr Hicks spread himself out in the grass and thought back to a brown café on a rainy day and what it had led him to.

AFTER

Gallons of tears, endless gallons of them, cascading down. The world through a mist: buildings, traffic, horrified faces.

Inside my new room in the new house in a new part of London, nothing but my old dry eyes, my old blank stare. No mist to obscure the old roses under the blue light.

How I wanted, in private, to squeeze out one tear of genuine sorrow, to exchange it for all those automatic gallons I had shed in the busy street.

'If it doesn't satisfy you, darling, why do you do it?'

'It occupies my time.'

'Ralph darling, you can't be so cynical.'

We were halfway through a second bottle of wine. We were talking seriously about my future.

'You *can't* be so negative.'

'I do it, that's all.'

'But children are involved, darling. Future people.'

I was aware, suddenly, that she was calling me 'darling'. It was a word she had never used before: I had been her 'love', her 'lamb'.

'I know they are—'

'I'm sorry I sound so pompous, Ralph, but what I mean is, it *must* be something more than a job to you—'

'It isn't. I have the facts in my head, I pass them on. I do it well enough.'

'I don't think you do. I think you could do it a great deal better. Your heart isn't in it.' She waited for me to speak. I shrugged. 'Ralph, it astonishes me, your attitude. I can't believe you don't care.'

I smiled and shrugged again.

AFTER

He told me his name was Mr Basil. Unusual, wasn't it? He had yet to meet the person who wasn't intrigued. 'I'm often asked if I've ever kept a fashion-house. You know, a couturier.' He made the word sound very French. 'And I always have to say no, I was born with this label, I didn't adopt it for business or pleasure. I was born Humphrey Basil and Humphrey Basil I will die.' He grinned abruptly and ran his index finger up his right sideboard. 'I regret to say that my life has been far from exotic, despite the impression I make on people.' His laugh was as abrupt as his grin. 'Oh, yes, deary me. All I've ever done is run this house, which I've owned from a tender age. Can you smell my cologne from where you're sitting?'

'Yes.'

'Too strong, is it? Too sweet?'

'No.'

'Subtle?'

'Yes. Yes, it is.'

'It's trying-out day, that's why I asked. The first time on. I like to have a variety of smells.' He grinned. 'A selection. I think this one *is* subtle, don't you?'

'Yes. Indeed.'

'Yes. I shall definitely add this one to my stock. Thank you. One meets all too few men these days, you know, who wear cologne. If they wear anything, it's usually some foul shaving-lotion. I curse the day the stuff was invented: it stings one's face so, besides being about as inviting as floor-polish. Still, I suppose it's preferable to good honest sweat, a commodity we English are strangely proud of.' He added, after a silence during which he looked at me intently, 'I am not a homosexual, by the way.'

'I didn't think—'

'Just to make matters clear. I hate misunderstandings. I may be a rarefied creature, but I hasten to add that my desires are all too drearily ordinary.'

The abrupt laugh ended in the abrupt grin. 'One or two of my past lodgers have tended to jump to conclusions and it's been really quite embarrassing, I must say, assuring them of my normal inclinations. And *such* an effort, as well, such an un-necessary effort. You know, the other morning I was waiting to be served at our local grocer's—you must try their port Stilton if you enjoy cheese—and I heard, quite distinctly, the word "pansy" being uttered. I saw immediately who the offender was. It was the new assistant. I walked over to the counter and I leaned across and I asked him to repeat what he'd said, but in a louder voice. He didn't reply. I like to think that he blushed under his spots. I then informed him politely – naturally – that I had been decorated in the war – I don't usually mention it, boasting's in terrible taste. I had helped to make the world a fit place for him and his kind to live in, I said, and would he please show me a little gratitude for doing it? He's a frightful child, anyway, quite frightful. More presentable-looking things have crawled out of my drains.'

I refused a Turkish cigarette.

'Well, back to business. You want the room?'

'Yes.'

'It costs a pound less than the others because it's really only a glorified attic. The wallpaper's excruciating, isn't it? The next time it's vacant I shall have it changed. I don't care what hours you keep or how many women you bring back. In fact, you can invite me to join in if you ever have too many on your hands.' The grin was more abrupt. 'My joke,' he explained. 'One other matter, if you find you have any complaints – which I'm only too sure you *will* have – don't bring them to me on Mondays or Fridays between six and seven, there's a good sport, will you? I'm massaged, you know, twice a week by a Mrs Schneider. She sees to it that the old body is kept up to the mark. You know? A rub-down with oil from head to foot, I can recommend it, there's nothing better. I haven't a care in the world when I'm on my rubber sheet.'

US

Early this morning, walking in the grounds, I tried to remember more of our life together. Near to panic, I stopped to calm myself. I said to someone: Please, please let those months come back to me, some fragments at least, some scenes.

So I tried to picture her. In her class, in the room, walking next to me.

Then, because even the picture wouldn't stay, the facts. Age:

twenty-seven. Hair: brown. Eyes: also brown, darker. Great cow's eyes.

She pinned photographs to the wall: an African child, a Sicilian peasant. They were there to remind us, she said.

'They don't really mingle – do they? – with the furniture.'

And for the kitchen, something more colourful: to the right of the oven, Seascape by June Pomeroy ($13\frac{1}{2}$); above the sink, Lovers In The Sun by Trevor Nesbit (14); and, below the rack for herbs, Swans In Park by James Berman (12), the only work to escape the steam and not buckle.

The word US yields nothing else. A sick taste comes to my mouth and the panic returns.

AFTER

I got off the bus. If I walk fast enough, I thought, and if I keep my head down as much as possible, no one will see these tears, the bloody senseless things.

I used my knuckles as windscreen-wipers.

Oh Christ, I thought, I'm still concerned what people think, I don't want them to see me in this state, I shall be embarrassed. As if it mattered. Mummy had brought up her Ralphie to be respectable, hadn't she?

I stood still. I laughed.

HER

Eight months of married bliss, eight whole months in her company. I looked up from my meal that evening and saw that she was watching me. No, watching *over* me, like a guardian angel; leading me, protecting me. I was something passive by comparison.

As we washed and dried the plates and glasses, her hip against mine, I suddenly wanted space. An easy explanation, of course: this stupid apology for a kitchen, no room to swing a cat, almost impossible to breathe with the two of us there —

And no, this wasn't my long room either. It had been so large and so much light had streamed in. No, it was hers too now, it belonged to both of us, we shared it. No, I couldn't lose myself here. Ellie (an E and an L and an L and an I and an E) was seeing to it that I was someone. She had made it her duty. Pigeons and roofs and television aerials.

'Ralph.'

She stood by the bed, naked.

'Ralph, love, please fuck me. I want you to.'

'Yes,' I said.

I fucked her.

AFTER

'He seemed perfectly normal when he arrived. Perfectly normal We had a long chat. He talked most interestingly. He struck me as educated at a glance. He obviously wasn't riff-raff, the usual type that comes here after rooms. And then to see him in the street, weeping and wailing, it was really a shock, you know.'

The doctor asked Mr Basil to be silent.

I did not hear them at the time: they were hands and arms and eyes. I hear them now.

HER

Her cow's eyes stared.

'What is it?' she asked.

'What does it look like?' I replied.

'It's a screen.'

'That's right. Clever Ellie.'

'But why?'

'What do you mean?'

'What I mean is, Ralph: why did you buy it?'

'I liked it. It appealed to me. If you move nearer you can see the design on it. It's St George fighting the dragon.'

She moved nearer. She touched it — her hand came forward, brushed against it. But then she withdrew her hand — quickly, decisively — as though afraid that the screen would bite it off.

'Ralph.' She smiled. 'You fool.'

'Am I?'

'Am I so much in your way?'

'Not at all. Nothing personal.'

But it was.

'You fool.'

AFTER

Even her death was a mess. Nothing comparatively subtle like drugs or gas. She had to hack, hack, hack.

HER

We ate in silence.

'You won't answer my questions?'

'What did you say?'

'Will you answer my questions?'

'There was only one. You asked why. The answer's easy. I don't know.'

'But you must.'

'But I don't.'

'It was as if you'd gone mad. They said.'

'They were right.'

'Were they misbehaving? Were they rude?'

'They were most attentive.'

'Then why?'

'I told you.'

'But you didn't, Ralph. Ralph, you didn't.'

'This rice is foul.'

'Don't eat it.'

'I shan't.'

'Surely you knew what you were doing. You could have controlled yourself.'

'I didn't.'

'Ralph, please. Please, Ralph, tell me.'

'Take your cow's eyes off me,' I shouted.

She threw a plate at the floor. It smashed.

'Be careful with the china,' I said.

'What you did today was senseless. You can't disguise it with jokes and insults.'

'I'm trying to.'

'They were children you screamed at.'

'They weren't gorillas.'

She picked up the pieces of china slowly and carefully.

'Ralph, if you tell me, perhaps I could help you. I *am* your wife.'

'Help me!'

'What you did—'

'What I did, what I did—'

'Ralph, my poor love—'

So I stood up and walked to the window and then walked back. I had a story in my head which was nothing like the truth. I told it to her—how, standing before my class, I had despaired of ever teaching them anything of any value. I had no power to change their lives, to inspire them. I was tired, thoroughly sick and tired, of making the effort. It was futile.

'We all feel like that at times,' she said.

'Do we?'

'Naturally. I feel desperate quite often.'

'No screams from you, though.'

'In a day or so, you'll be surprised it ever happened.'

Julius Caesar and his army had entered the classroom, had pulled the light bulbs from their sockets, had disposed of the desks like so much undergrowth, had hacked off the children's heads.

Out they came, the words of comfort. Ellie, the comforter, spoke. She stroked my hair and then she kissed my face and hands.

Love was making the world go round again. All was concord.

AFTER

Mr Basil's new lodger allowed them to lift him. Their hands were both gentle and firm. They led him slowly down stair after stair. They drove off with him. Mr Basil's new lodger, who appreciated cheese, had not yet tasted the port Stilton.

HER

The music was loud. I went behind my screen.

Minutes later, she turned off the record. She called out, 'Ralph, come and talk to me.'

I said nothing.

'Are you going to talk to me?'

I stayed silent, but I got up and went across to where she was sitting. I sat opposite her.

'Are you going to?'

I shrugged. 'What about?'

'Am I such a fool?' she asked.

'You know yourself better than I do.'

'Do you think I'm a fool?'

'I don't know what I think about you.'

'Why *did* you marry me?'

'That will take some answering.'

'You could say why.'

'Oh no, I couldn't.'

'You could.'

'I couldn't, you could; I couldn't, you could; I—'

'I love you,' she broke in.

'What a strange thing to say.'

'I mean it.'

'I didn't contradict you.'

'I wanted to make it clear.'

'You've succeeded.'

'I don't know what to say to you, I don't know what—' She began to cry. She sniffed loudly. 'Will you listen to me?'

'All ears.'

'Will you?'

'As I said.'

'I want us to be happy.'

After a pause I said, 'I listened.'

'We've got to be.'

'What do you suggest?'

'I wish I was clever, Ralph. I wish I could amuse you and make you respect me.'

'Stop grovelling.'

'I'm a big dumb thing, I suppose. I can't exist without your love.'

'Shut your silly bloody mouth,' I shouted.

'I won't. I can't.'

She sobbed.

I went to the kitchen and picked up the plastic bucket from under the sink. I placed it at her feet.

'I hope that's large enough.'

Still sobbing, she passed me and flew at the screen. She tore at it, screaming 'This. This.'

She pushed it over and fell on it, her claws still striking.

'Poor St George,' I said. 'Poor dragon. What a mess you've made of them.'

'Oh Ralph,' she said, 'have me.'

Her cure for every ill. 'No, I don't want to.' I walked out.

AFTER

'If you have a moment, Mr Hicks,' said Mrs Dinsdale, 'I'd like, if I may, to have a few words with you.'

We were in the hall. Ellie, covered up and on a stretcher, had been taken out.

I nodded.

'Come to my office.' I followed her down to the basement. She sat behind her desk.

'I don't know how to say this,' she began. She coughed genteelly. 'I am, of course, very sorry for you.'

I nodded again.

'But I must add that it's my opinion, Mr Hicks, that people who –' she searched for a word – 'that people who dispose of themselves are as inconsiderate as they're wicked. All that blood in my bathroom. I shan't ask you to foot the bill for decoration, but I shall ask you to leave.'

I could do nothing but nod.

'I suppose wicked was too strong a word. Perhaps unnatural is nearer the mark. Your wife, Mr Hicks, went against nature. However, as I was saying, this house of mine does have a good name and I don't want any more troubles under my roof and there's an end of it.'

She waited for me to speak. I merely looked at her.

'Can't you say anything? I take it your nods mean that you will comply with my wishes? Very well.' She rose, smoothing her skirt down. 'I always thought there was something odd about your wife. Her father, that general or colonel or whatever –'

I mouthed the word 'Major'.

'Yes, well, major or whatever. He was odd, too, if you ask me. He made an obscene suggestion to me at your wedding reception. He was very drunk.' She paused.

'He told me he would like to bite my nipples off.'

We stared at each other.

I removed her blouse and her brassière. She stepped out of her shoes as I removed her skirt. I removed her panties.

She lay on a divan. I dropped my trousers and fucked Mrs Ruby Dinsdale.

When she was dressed she said, 'You'll oblige me by finding another place to live at your earliest convenience.'

4

I want to get out of myself.

I shall begin with him. He is Ellie's friend. Was, was. He *was* Ellie's friend. She once said he was her inspiration.

Let me be her inspiration for a while. Let me utter those tired phrases; let me be anxious to shock and amuse.

I am so truly sick of myself that it will be pleasant to be Bernard Proctor.

And so I start:

Welcome to Auntie Bernard's palatial parlour and mind your head on the chandelier—it hangs low, like all the best things.

Nothing gives me greater pleasure than to talk about myself. I once said to Mums—after she'd gone over to Rome, that is—that if I ever went too, the priest would never get away, I'd have him fixed with my glittering eye, he'd be in that box all day and night while I had a good old wallow. *You have been warned.*

I could never compete with Mums in the personality stakes. I say that in all humility. She was an extraordinary creature, she really was. Had there been more like her, I feel sure that England would have had a revolution. Blood would have flowed in the streets and heads would have tumbled. There must have been dozens of shop assistants—from Harrods and Fortnum's and many points between—who would have been willing to man the barricades, if only for the chance of taking a pot-shot at her. She was not the world's most lovable lady.

She never arrived at places, she descended on them. Swooped down, rather. She swooped down on to my school a few times – yes, it *was* public and yes, the masters *did* fondle our bums while they were correcting our Latin – and every time she came she appeared to be a bit less real. You could smell her scent for days after. All the other boys were terribly envious – 'I say, Proctor, your mother is a *riot*' – and some of them even told me, it was intended as a compliment, that they kept her in mind when they were exercising their wrists. I told her so years later and she smiled sweetly and said she was deeply touched. She omitted to tell me that she had seduced our house-captain on one of her visits. He told me himself.

Mums's father – she called him Dads – owned a salon in Mayfair and left her a good deal of money. He died – and so did his wife, Mums's Mums – before I was born. They were killed in a car accident near Monte Carlo. I remember once standing with her in silence – her silences were so rare that I can't help but remember them – at the crossing where it had happened.

That was our only holiday together and a pretty fatal one it was, too. As I have no doubt mentioned before, I caught my first dose of clap – in the place where men are supposed to catch it – from a chorus boy with liquid eyes, and I had to give up champagne and devote long hours of every day to fun with my water-pistol. A French farce, that one was, to end them all.

However, back to Mums. My father, who lived off her for years, left her for an actress when I was ten. 'Is she a famous actress, Mums?' I asked. 'Goodness no, dear,' she replied. 'She sounds distinctly tuppenny-ha'penny. They're living in a boarding-house. She's a strolling player by the sound of it.' So, after that, Father's lady-love – and I think he *must* have loved her because we heard from our cook, who had heard it from someone else, that he had actually taken a job somewhere – after that, Father's girl friend was always referred to as The Strolling

Player (Mums adored giving people names) with one or two variations like The Pocket Bernhardt or The Thespian. Father became — and there were no variations for him — The Bastard, although this was abbreviated to The B in letters.

Mums's letters! I have most of them to this day. When I'm really in the dumps, when my pecker is in need of lifting up, I undo the blue ribbon and read some of the more hilarious passages. Her letters may not be in the Lady Mary Wortley Montagu class (Confession Number One: I've never read Her Ladyship) but, by God, they *are* funny. One sentence and there she is, as vividly and monstrously alive as ever. I once wrote to tell her that I'd seen my first opera — *Figaro*. Her reply — from the Royal Picardy, Le Touquet — said she was so pleased I had developed a taste for opera, which was such a very civilized pastime, but would I give her my assurance that I'd never, on any account, become an admirer of the monstrous Wagner. She was not objecting to the velvet-jacketed gentleman's charming political leanings, because — I'm ashamed to say — she was a bit of a fascist herself. No, her objections were purely aesthetic. 'It's all so long and everyone looks so disgustingly robust. There are no clothes to speak of in Wagner. An evening spent in contemplation of a well-filled shift is not my idea of delight.'

Another time I wrote saying that I wanted to be a poet when I grew up. I even sent her some of my poems, which were all very homo in theme — wince-making words like 'lad' kept cropping up and there were references to 'lovely limbs' and 'dew-glistening thighs'. I'd describe the style now as Scoutmaster Tasteful Classical. Nasty repressed stuff it was *and* absolute non-sense — I mean, if your thighs were glistening with dew you'd be dead from pneumonia within the week, wouldn't you? Anyway, 'I want to be a poet,' I wrote. 'If you keep writing,' she answered, 'there is no reason why you shouldn't become another Keats or Shelley. Only don't die as they did. So young, the pair of them, starving in that appalling garret — their Mumses must have been shattered at losing them. You are not to die young — that is an order!'

But mostly the letters contained gossip—who was doing what to whom and where. They made wonderful bedtime reading in the dormitory. Mums's ears must have worked overtime under her blue rinse. And all the lovers she had—I was kept up to date on that score, too. She made my life seem very drab—there were no sun-tanned youths sending me red roses or smiling beguilingly at me from behind a glass of chilled white wine. Far from it. A burst of acne had hit my poor face, which only made my pathetic attempts to entice the heartiest and hairiest boy in the school into my maiden bed the more doomed to certain failure. The Proctor stomach turned over every time he appeared—clad or otherwise, but especially otherwise. Twenty years later we met in Bruton Street: he was even heartier and hairier, sporting the most ridiculous handle-bar moustache. 'Let's have a pint of bitter together, old man,' he said. So I said I only drank gin, a bottle of which I had in my bijou abode some ten minutes' walk away: would *that* be acceptable? 'Just the job. We can have a good old chinwag in comfort.' He strode along beside me. No sooner had we entered the flat than his great hairy hand pounced on to my bottom and fixed itself there. 'May I, old man?' he asked. 'An't please your worship,' I said back, and I tried to drop a grateful curtsy, which perplexed him rather. That was the extent of our chinwag. When the doing was done, he shook my hand and slapped my back and marched off into obscurity again.

But, as usual, I digress. I was talking about Mums's letters, wasn't I? Well, for many, many years they were my only contact with her. If I had a mother it was by long distance. It was probably a blessing in disguise, as they say. I was monstrous enough without her; *with* her I'd have been totally unbearable. The mere thought of my years at Oxford—oh, them gleaming spires!—makes me shudder. It's not the outrageous clothes and the outrageous behaviour so much as our absolute and total ignorance of the way most people in England were living at the time. While we were all whooping it up and spending small fortunes on drag parties, hungry men were marching to London from the north and in some parts of this sceptr'd isle a tin shack was considered a desirable property. God rot us for not noticing and not caring.

However, I'm jumping the gun again. I came down to the great metropolis and I continued to live it up: my social conscience was still some months away. I worked, in the loosest possible sense, for a publisher – translating engineering manuals and such into readable English. I spent all my earnings – and some of my allowance from Mums – at theatres and restaurants and then, to round off a perfect day, on guardsmen. Those pre-war prices were most reasonable: two-and-six for handicrafts and as little sometimes as five shillings for a full-scale operation, complete with trimmings. I must have had dozens of them – one of my friends swore he'd seen two account cards in my wallet, one for a department store and the other for Chelsea barracks. It was like a drug for me, except that the effects always wore off so quickly. I often trudged out in search of my injection in weather that would have deterred Nanook of the North.

It was on just such a search that I met Jim, the love of my life. Oh dear, it does sound so sordid, doesn't it? Still, the truth is the truth and this particular Miss Capulet met her Mr Montague in a dark and gloomy lavatory in the vicinity of Blackfriars Bridge. It was *so* dark and gloomy, in fact, that we had to walk out into the street to see what we both looked like. We saw and we fell and from that moment romance bloomed. How many couples can boast such an enchanted beginning?

He was barely literate but he taught me a good few values. So many people today assume that having an education is like having a passport to understanding and decency. It's a myth, I fear. Jim couldn't help being anything but decent and kind yet writing a letter was, for him, as daunting an ordeal as swimming the Channel. He put me in my place several times. 'Can't you ever behave naturally? Why do you have to speak in that stupid voice? You're talking to *me,* you know.'

We decided we'd share my flat and he insisted on paying half the rent from the meagre wages he earned as a carpenter's apprentice. He had great trouble getting away from his parents, particularly his mother, old Ada Burris, who was so ghastly that La Divina Goacher seems almost human by comparison. I was called into her presence one cheerless Sunday afternoon and I must say I felt distinctly uneasy as I climbed the stairs at Empress Dwellings. The squalor! Ada, Sid, Evie and Jim all lived together in two rooms at the very top. There was no electricity and one water tap in the forecourt served the entire house. The main reason for my uneasiness, though, was because I was convinced that I was about to play the role of the future bride being inspected by the groom's family. I certainly did get stared at that day, but only Ada—whose eyes were the kind that wool had never been pulled over—guessed what was going on between her son and the gentleman caller. We ate vinegar-soaked cucumber sandwiches and drank tea the colour of ox-blood as Ada prattled on about how pleased she was that her boy had made such a good friend and one, what's more, who had a shilling or two to spare; it was such an honour for them to have—beg pardon the expression—a toff come to call and sit down and take a bite with them. I tried to appear as relaxed as I could. Her choicest phrases were all repeated at full volume for the benefit of Sid, on whose deaf side she had cleverly seated herself. Evie, who was fat and plain and wore a surgical boot, looked at me as though I was a creature from another world—which, in a way, I was. I caught her eye once or twice and I could sense how insincere and forced my smile was. I felt so ashamed: she sat there, a lump, marked out by Mother Nature to be unloved, casting looks of adoration at her young brother. She obviously hadn't realized—and Jim afterwards bore this out—that she was doomed to a life of drudgery. Ada ran the family with words, Evie with deeds. Ages later, she wrote to tell me of her mother's death. I invited her to dinner. She came, and—at the age of forty-seven—drank her first glass of wine. She choked to begin with but after that, she said, it went down very nicely, although she couldn't see herself making a habit of it. We talked about Jim, she was proud of him being brave but she would have preferred him alive for all that. She would see her deaf old father to his last rest and then, who knew, she'd have to do more than taking in ironing and sewing to earn her daily bread, wouldn't she? I said she must go home by taxi. She complained of the extravagance. I insisted. In the street, I hailed a cab. Clump, clump, clump down the stairs she came. We stood for a moment on the doorstep, embarrassed. She cupped my face in her hands and kissed me. She waved as the taxi drew off. I somehow managed to close the front door. I bent over, I remember, and I wept. I have seldom in my life been so honoured.

I seem to have strayed again, as is my wont. I love that phrase, don't you—as is my wont? Well, the evening after my Sunday visit, Jim came round to the flat carrying a small suitcase which, he said, contained all his possessions. His farewell to the Dwellings, I soon learned, had not been pleasant: decidedly *un*pleasant, in fact, with Ada screaming loudly from a balcony. 'I don't want a bleeding brown-hatter for a son' was the phrase that rang melodiously in his ears all the way to Aldgate station. She had, it seemed, goaded him—by way of scarcely veiled references—into blurting out the truth about us. She had settled for 'brown-hatter' only after exploring all the other possibilities: Nancy, pansy, arse-hole prodder. (She obviously couldn't conceive of her son being passive.) At one point in her recital she had even invoked the Almighty. 'Do you think the Lord gave you a pair of bollocks', she wanted to know, 'so as you could let them run to waste?'

And so began—as they say in memoirs—the happiest period of my life. To start with, I treated him a bit like Eliza Doolittle—you know, introducing him ever so gently to what we privileged mortals call culture. Bedtime readings from the classics and so forth. I once took him to the ballet—the stress is on the second syllable—and I was so proud of him: he laughed loudly all the way through some terrible piece, a positive feast of fish-net, called *The Triumph of Death*. As soon as the serpent began to rape the heroine, we had to leave: accompanied, I might add, by sibilant cries of 'Philistines!' Oh, I adored him that evening. The theatre was filled with earnest queens all saying '*So* profound',

'Serge has never offered us anything as meaningful as this' and there was Jim, bright-eyed with disbelief, trusting his native intelligence and coming to the right conclusion.

Re-enter Mums. She rang one afternoon and Jim answered the phone—he was still unaccustomed to it, so he shouted into the mouthpiece, holding the receiver a good foot away from him. '*Who* was that?' asked Mums as soon as she realized that her darling boy was on the other end of the line. 'Have you got a workman in?' When I'd recovered from the fit of hysterics brought on by her question I managed to reply 'Not at the moment' and immediately collapsed again. We arranged to meet at the Ritz for tea.

We met. Picture the scene. Me, in my most discreet apparel, pretending to listen intently as Mums—little finger crooked above the handle of her cup, her free hand soaring and drooping —describes the last few months on Capri. She finishes. I embark on a slab of walnut cake. It is time now for seriousness.

MUMS. You were quite extraordinary on the telephone today, dear. Your Mums wondered if you were really of sound mind.

ME. Yes, Mums, I'm sorry. It was a private joke, you see.

MUMS. With the man who nearly deafened me?

ME. Yes, Mums. Mums—(I concentrate on the crumbs on my plate, arranging them into patterns)—I have something to tell you.

MUMS. Tell me then.

ME. It might come as a shock to you.

MUMS. Does anything shock me, dear? I doubt it.

ME. This might. It's my private life—

MUMS. Yes, dear—what about it?

ME. It's my tendencies—

MUMS. What about them?

ME. (I cough away the phlegm that has gathered in my throat. A whisper escapes from me—) I'm a homosexual.

MUMS. I know you are, dear. What about it?

ME. How *could* you know, Mums?

MUMS. How *couldn't* I, you mean. It's as plain as a pikestaff, dear. You were always—what's the expression?—a sensitive plant. I'm glad you are: there are far too many brutes in this world. Those beautiful poems you sent me from school, they told me the whole story. Who wants to be normal anyway? The greatest artists were all homosexual—

ME. Now, Mums—

MUMS. Of course they were. Don't argue. This is one subject I *do* know about. Michelangelo, Leonardo, Shakespeare, Beethoven—all of them.

ME. The man who answered the phone, Mums, is my lover.

MUMS. But he sounded so common—

ME. He was born in the East End—

MUMS. You *must* be careful. Being different is perfectly all right, nothing wrong with it at all, but you *must* be careful in your choice of friends. You can't go scouring the gutters, dear. Working people are all very well, they perform a useful service, but it's absolutely necessary to keep one's distance from them. They take liberties, otherwise; they betray one. Follow my advice, dear, and find yourself someone from a good school. Or from Sandhurst—I'd like to think of you married to a handsome young officer.

ME. I love him, Mums.

MUMS. Now, dear, control yourself. You can't take him to the best parties—you know that, don't you? Let's change the subject. Have you heard from The Bastard?

ME. No. Should I have done?

MUMS. I simply wondered. I suppose he *is* still with The Strolling Player?

ME. I suppose so, Mums.

And the touching scene drew to its close.

Where Mums failed, Hitler succeeded. The war began and Jim went away. The army, to my amazement, declined the offer of my services. Blood pressure. I remained in London, working for the fire service.

I shan't inflict all the details of my Great Sorrow on you. I've nothing but contempt for people who do it to me. 'I do not wish to hear,' I say to them, ever so brusquely. What I *will* say, though, is that I was a different man when I was with Jim, I wasn't always a parody pansy. I lived quite simply; I even spoke simply, which took some doing.

Memory's a great one with her little tricks, isn't she? It all seems so idyllic from this distance. Would we have been able to continue in that happy, uneventful way? It's a chilling thought — granted more time together we might have become (like so many do) a couple of bickerers: 'queens' means 'scenes'. Or the kind who ask each other twenty-four hours every day: 'Do you still love me? You *do*, don't you?' Or the kind who can enjoy each other only when they're indulging in threesomes. Or the kind who just break up. To return to the actual plot. I received that card from Germany and went into a decline. 'Only disconnect' became my motto. I saw no one. Another period I look back on with a shudder: I floundered in self-pity, I realize now. I took to injection-hunting once more. There was plenty of scope, the war hadn't ended. I was obliged in several doorways. I lost interest when I was spoken to: I preferred a nod or a wink; I preferred it quick and brutal.

I hadn't seen Mums since the tête-à-tête over the Earl Grey. News had reached her in faraway Suffolk of Jim's death. Could she call on me with a gentleman friend? 'A lover, Mums?' 'No dear, quite the reverse. A priest.' She rang off before I could ask why she was bringing a priest to see me. I soon discovered the reason.

I don't think I can do justice to Father Flynn. He was seven feet tall, he had protruding teeth, hands like sides of beef and eyes out on stalks. Centuries of inbreeding are responsible for you, I thought as he sent the chandelier tinkling. Mums, you're a marvel, you've brought this clown to cheer me up. Alas no, she hadn't. Father Flynn was a deadly serious specimen, it quickly became clear. He held my hand in his — he covered it, rather — and patted it as gently as he could. 'Have you something in your eye?' I asked and then it dawned on me that he wasn't squinting but giving me the Clerical Look of Sympathy. (You know the one—you peer closely at your victim and you nod slowly, as if to say 'You don't have to speak. I understand.') 'Could I possibly have my hand back?' I asked eventually. 'I have to prepare something dainty for the trolley.' 'Of course, of course.' 'You're about to back into the fireplace,' I said, 'so would you kindly sit down?' And I added, wickedly, 'For Christ's sake.'

I heard, from the kitchen, the lilt of the Emerald Isle: 'He's obviously been under a great deal of stress.' 'And a great many Irish labourers, too,' I called out. What is known as a pregnant silence ensued.

'Tea up!' I chirped brightly as I entered with a plate of fish-paste sandwiches. 'I don't want to see any of these left.' Which was perfectly true: Jim had bought a jar of the disgusting stuff five years before and it had remained in the Proctor pantry the entire time. Waste not, want not—Father Flynn's visit was heaven-sent in one respect at least. Nineteen of the twenty sandwiches prepared found their way into the priestly intestines; Mums bit into the remaining one and then, with horror etched large across her features, returned it to the plate.

Pregnant silences seemed to be the order of the day. To relieve the monotony I said, 'Mums, whatever is the matter? You're not your usual old self at all.'

'I certainly am not, dear. I'm a new woman.'

'A new woman? Does that mean you have a good lover?'

'In a sense, dear, in a sense. I have Jesus Christ.'

'Mrs Proctor has been re-born in the spirit,' said Father Flynn.

Oh no, I thought, the silly cow *hasn't* become a Holy Roman. Not *that*.

'My life has meaning at last,' she said. 'I have come out of the wilderness.'

'Mrs Proctor is at peace with herself. Joy is in her heart.'

I looked at Father Flynn. 'Is it? She doesn't appear very joyful. Tell me, Father, has she confessed to you?'

'She has, my son.'

'I bet it was entertaining, wasn't it?'

Those Irish eyes didn't smile. 'Your mother has taken a very serious decision. She has cleansed herself.'

'Yes, Bernard, it's true. I am clean.' A meaningful pause. Something's up, I said to myself, something *is* up. 'You could be clean, too. Father Flynn is ready and willing to help you.'

'Are you, Father?'

'I am, my son. Shall I go on, Mrs Proctor?' Mums nodded. It was all very strange. 'Your mother has told me about your problem. Believe me, I *do* understand, I know what agonies you must go through.'

'Do you, Father? I'm a trifle confused—which problem of mine are you referring to?'

'Would you rather we discussed it man to man? If there's another room—'

I brought him to heel. 'You have not answered my question, Father. Which problem?'

'*The* one.'

I was remorseless by now. '*The* one?'

'Yes. Your *physical* one.'

'But *which* physical one?' I asked sweetly.

I realized suddenly that my decline was over; my appetite for living was back. But then Mums brought my fun and games to a halt by saying, 'I told Father Flynn about your queer leanings, Bernard.'

'That's right. And I *do* understand, I know what agonies you must go through,'

'How do you know, Father?'

'I have been called to.' The blandness of it!

'Oh, I see. You spoke with such certainty I wondered if you too were in the club.'

'Which club?'

Mums to the rescue once more: 'My son is being offensive, Father. Take no notice. Do behave yourself, Bernard.'

'This *is* my flat, Mums,' I reminded her. 'Would you mind telling me the purpose of your visit?'

'What a silly question, dear. We haven't seen each other for years. I came to find out how you were—'

'Then why did you bring the clergy with you?'

'Because, dear, because I want you to experience the same happiness that I now have. Losing your friend—'

'The one you advised me to throw over? The one I couldn't take with me to the best parties?' I launched into an aria of obscenities; Ada Burris herself could not have surpassed me. I told Mums that I despised and hated her: her shallowness and stupidity, her vanity, her snobbishness, her cruelty. But most of all I loathed her for her hypocrisy, for the ease with which she assumed it was possible to wipe away fifty years of thoughtlessness by offering herself up to some senseless Deity.

I stood there snorting like a bull. Mums said nothing. I glared at Father Flynn.

'God is doing his work inside you,' he said. 'You have just shed a load of bitterness.'

I bawled at them to leave. They went out crossing themselves, like Mrs Goacher's mad lodger.

After that joyous outburst it seemed only right and proper that Bernard Proctor should prove to the world that he wasn't as thoughtless as he had accused his mother of being. He wanted to be of use to someone.

So—back we go into the first person—I applied for a post that I'd seen advertised in a weekly journal. I went before this forbidding board and explained to them why I considered myself the best person there was to take evening classes in English literature a stone's throw from the sound of Bow Bells. I rattled off the names of all the authors I'd read, from Beowulf onwards. I kept my legs apart and made absolutely sure that not a single hairpin was dropped.

I can honestly say that the job I have somehow managed to cling on to all these years has given me more satisfaction than anything else in life, except for those few months in You-know-who's company. My business and my pleasure have been kept strictly apart, although I've been sorely tempted many times—as you can well imagine, working where I do. I have never dallied with any of the golden youths who have passed through my metaphorical hands.

I haven't finished with Mums yet, I'm afraid. I heard from her – or rather, from the put-upon nurse who was looking after her – for the last time. The pain-killing drugs she was taking had made her temporarily deranged: the nurse had discovered her in the sitting-room one morning pissing (Nursie, of course, said 'passing water') into the Meissen tea-cups. Mrs Proctor was now in hospital.

Mums and her wayward son made their last contact.

'Have they told you what's wrong with me?'

'Yes,' I said.

'Frightful place to have it in, isn't it?' It was – she had cancer of the rectum. 'I laugh about it when it isn't hurting me.'

I simply couldn't believe it: a courageous Mums, a dignified Mums? And I performed an about-face, too: I asked her forgiveness for what I'd said. It was granted. She also apologized for trying to convert me. She knew now it was a personal matter, it had to rise up in you, it had to come from your heart. As far as she was concerned, sweet Jesus was the only man who had ever made any sense to her in this bloody world.

I stayed with her until she died, two days later. A priest gave her the last rites. Her face was serene.

Out in the street, I felt my old hatred seething up – what right had she to die so well? People whose lives had been decent and good and blessed with love went out screaming their heads off. Mums the selfish, Mums the cruel, Mums the every vice you could put a name to, had died as beautifully as any saint.

I came home to the gin bottle and then I went cruising. I prowl the streets and scatter the good seed on the hand. Many an old haunt was revisited that night. A Negro said he could give me twelve inches if I gave *him* five pounds. I had little in cash – would he accept a cheque? No, he said, he hadn't yet opened a bank account. *Ciao.*

After which, it was hard by the shore of silver-streaming Thames and into the most notorious lavatory in the south-west area. Was it empty? Almost, but not quite. One tall gentleman at the very end. Yes, just the job, tall and broad with it. A strong profile. A handsome, rugged face. And what a nice smile, so full and generous, such fine white teeth. And *what* a lovely appendage, not up to the promised five pounds' worth but enough — *more* than enough — for gin-soaked, motherless, Jim-less Bernard. Notes were compared — do you like mine? I like *yours* — and hands explored and then I found myself in a van, seated next to an old queen, the lines on whose face had been partly obscured with orange make-up and down whose cheeks enormous tears — of the kind one only ever seems to see in films — rolled and rolled and rolled. Before we drove away at midnight, we had been joined by four others.

In the dingy court-room the following morning I stood, unwashed and unshaven, and listened as the magistrate described me as 'a shameful man' and Police-Constable Jenkins, Ronald Percival, stated in a loud, clear voice that I had made a grossly indecent proposal to him. (Marry me, Police-Constable Jenkins, Ronald Percival, marry me, do.) I said I was a clerk and paid my fine (yes, they would accept a cheque) and I walked slowly home, hoping against hope that the authorities wouldn't find out and take my job away from me. They didn't. It's some kind of a miracle that no one read the little item at the bottom of page three in that Sunday newspaper, next to the advertisement that promised relief from constipation. Or perhaps someone did read it, but took pity on me and decided not to protest. That person — it might even be persons — has my gratitude, I do assure him. Or her. It was another miracle that I passed out on the kitchen floor the night I heard about poor Ellie — I know the police don't get up to those wicked tricks any more, but something equally nasty might have happened with me in that condition.

I was the chief mourner at Mums's funeral. Oh, that hateful ritual! When it's my turn, as they say, please Someone, just shove me arse-upwards into a dustbin and set me alight. Then you can

scatter me to the winds. Thanks. Meanwhile, back at the graveyard: when it was all over, I was stopped by an elderly man. He
had receding sandy hair and there were gaps in his dentures –
his breath was so foul that I had to brush a hand against my nose
whenever he spoke. 'Hullo, old chap,' he said. 'I'm your father.
I don't suppose you wish to speak to me.' 'Hullo,' I said. We
shook hands. 'I came to pay my last respects. Ended up R.C., did
she?' 'Yes.' 'I saw when the funeral was from the back page of
The Times. I haven't much work on at the moment, business is
always bad at this time of the year, so I thought I'd come, pay
my last respects, see her off as it were.' 'Yes' was still all I could
say. 'Well then, I'd better get back to Alice.' 'The – actress?' (I'd
nearly said 'The Strolling Player'.) 'Yes, she *was* on the boards.
She gave it up. I've been the breadwinner for many a long year.'
You – a breadwinner? – in that shabby raincoat, in those cracked
shoes ... I reached for my wallet, automatically. 'Christ no,
old chap, I'm not on the scrounge. I must be off.' And off he
fled.

And there you have me, if you'll pardon the expression. I'm
very out of date, aren't I? I scarcely fit into this modern society.
I can't get used to freedom; I suppose I crave the martyr's crown.
The dirty back-streets and the stinking lavatories are my hunting-
grounds; they're fit settings for humiliation: the clubs and bars,
with everyone so open and happy, they only oppress me. They
tear at my heart because I remember what I had. And anyway,
I always did hate my kind *en masse*.

It's most unreasonable. But, if I'm honest, I have to confess that
I enjoy putting on a show for all you normal specimens. It gives
me pleasure. I'm one of that wretched number who thrive on
pain. It keeps me going; it makes me tick. And, like a child, I
expect you to applaud me.

So clap your hands now. My glittering eye is getting spots
before it. I need my rest, I'm not as young as I was, and I *do* have
a class tomorrow. England is still a terrible place, class is still
warring against class; whatever they say, there is still some darkness shrouding this land of ours. I believe in what I do, and I hope

and pray I do it well. I hope I lighten a few dark corners in my children's minds.

'You're too much on edge to be a country girl,' my mother said to me one day. 'You should take life calmly like I do, Mary.' I never could, I tried, because from when I was very young I seemed to be cursed with nerves; I had to clench my fists tight sometimes and keep my feet firm beneath me and say to myself, 'Steady now, Mary Longhurst'—otherwise, I swear, my top would have blown off. I was put out by simple things that my mother, Ralphie's grandmother that is, took in her stride. She was heavy and slow and calm and I liked nothing better in the evenings than to lie on the mat with my head against her skirt: she would pinch my cheek every now and then to check that I hadn't dozed off; it sounds funny, I don't believe in magic, but even today—all this time afterwards—I smelt her hands again. It *is* funny, I know, but that smell *did* come to me as I sat here half-asleep in my chair—I can't describe it, I was never a one for words, but there was onion in it and a herb I've forgotten the name of and cow's udders, which is the funniest part. Daft thing that I am, I took a peep behind me to see if my mother was in the room. I need hardly say she wasn't. Milly brought me back to earth again by wheeling in our supper.

When things went wrong, when George—my husband that is, Ralphie's father—began to complain of my little mind, I used to think of that time on the farm and it brought me a bit of peace. My mother was always around to stop my nerves jumping with a sensible word or a strong grip on my shoulders. She had it in her to insult me too, I can't deny—but then she never left terra firma, no worries were big enough to disturb her nature; and she had it in her to wound too, but I know it was by accident, it wasn't done in the way George did it. I used to think as well of the wonderful meals she cooked in her old black range and that *I* could never equal when *I* started cooking, however much I told

myself not to panic, it would come out right if I steadied myself—
her roasts and her cakes and her apple pie with cloves and lemon
peel. Ralphie was very partial as a boy to his grandmother's
gooseberry tart.

My mother was boss in the house, but then she maintained that
my father had the two fields and the barns and the sheds to himself, he was lord and master there, so she was going to rule over
her roost without any interference — Mrs Longhurst's cottage was
one place in these parts you didn't dare enter with muck on your
boots, she always said. Her housework was usually done by nine
in the morning. When we were living above the shop — George
and Ralphie and me — I would count myself fortunate sometimes
if I'd finished mine by five in the afternoon. But there, I had no
system. My mother had a system, and so has Milly. When I
cleaned and polished I could never see an end to it. It was like
being in a jungle, which I know sounds funny, and I couldn't
find my way out: I often needed a good cry to bring me back to
the fact that I was only in my home and I only had to stay calm.

I went to the village school. It took me much longer than any
of the others to learn to read and write. The teacher, a Mrs
Christmas — what a silly name, we used to say: 'she can't be
wicked with a handle like that,' my father said — she showed
great patience with me, she took real pains on my behalf. Without her, I mean to say, I'd be a proper dunce and no mistake. I
was proud of my Ralphie being able to read so much, I know the
value of education even though I had my troubles with words
and facts and figures.

My schooling was over when I was fourteen and my mother
sent me up to the big house to wait at table for the bishop and
his lady — I was to come home with no airs and graces, she
warned me, expecting Irish linen on my bed and fine silver alongside my dinner plate; I wasn't to forget my beginnings as so
many girls did when they got themselves a sniff of a better life.
I promised her faithfully I'd return home the same Mary Longhurst; living in a bishop's house wouldn't turn me into any
stuck-up city miss, I said. She gave me her quick peck on the

forehead – it was the nearest she ever got to showing her feelings; she hated to see people, she said, slobbering over each other in full view of man and beast – and she told me not to panic, to take things easy as *she* did, the natural way, the way the Lord wanted His creatures to be. I've forgotten all about my time with the bishop – except that he liked his tipple, as the saying goes, and had trouble with his wind; not rudely, nothing offensive, it was his food repeating on him – but I often recall my first night away from home. My new room was tiny, it had no fancy pieces in it, but even so it was grander than anything I had ever seen before. I lay between those icy sheets and wondered what would happen to me if I was shouted at or not shown patience. It would be terrible if I screamed or cried in front of a man of God. But I didn't, I'm happy to report, the entire time I was there: of course, I *did* come near to blowing my top, I have been near all my life to doing so, but my mother's words would always save me in the nick of time. The old bishop died and the new one brought his own staff with him – they were hated for miles around, that lot – and I went home to the farm again. I was ashamed of myself for feeling out of place, but the truth was, I did, and my mother said it showed in my looks and I had better find myself a position before I pined away completely, I would put the cows off their stroke if they caught a glimpse of me.

I went from job to job for a good ten years or more, from one grand house to another, and then this family I was with, they decided to return to London, the country bored them, they said. They took me with them, I was twenty-nine, I'd never been further than twenty miles from the house I'd been born in, it was quite a wrench, having to say goodbye to my mother and father and the folk in the village I cared for. I had to take myself off to the toilet once the train was in motion and I sobbed and sobbed and hoped that the wheels going round would cover up the noise I was making. Three of my best lace handkerchiefs were soaked through before I gave myself a talking-to and went back to the compartment.

Even after a whole week I had my doubts as to whether I'd ever accustom myself to London – there seemed no limit to its size: one street followed into another and you no sooner found yourself on a patch of green than you were back on concrete once again. I had shocking nightmares in which tall buildings fell on me, or I couldn't breathe because there was no space to speak of between them: it sounds funny now but it had simply never occurred to me that London could be so dark and dirty. It was summer when I arrived and everyone was complaining of the heat; it is the way of people in London, I've noticed, to always complain about the heat or the cold.

I met George. I first saw him when I was in the kitchen with Cook going through the day's menu – she called it the 'me and you', we had some laughs together, the two of us – and I turned on my heel and there he was, come to deliver the groceries. He wore a grubby white overall and the sight of him swept me off my feet, I swear it did. The second time he came I was at the sink, singing my head off – I liked to open my throat a bit in those days – and he told me to go on when I stopped, it was a pretty sound I made, although he hadn't more than half a clue as to what the words meant. It was a country song I'd been singing, I said, and I'd been sung it by my Mam. 'Your Mam's your mother, is she?' he asked me and I said 'Yes' and then I became cheeky and said to him who did he think she was. Then he looked about him and went to the door and opened it slightly to see if anyone was there and then he asked me – straight out and bold as brass – when my free evening was. 'Thursday,' I said. 'What time are you finished?' 'As near to six as makes no difference,' I said, cheeky again. 'I'll be here on the dot,' he promised me and then he was gone. I was in a flutter that Thursday, I must say; even at four in the afternoon I was having butterflies as the saying goes. I thought to myself: he won't come, he was just teasing, he was flirting with me that was all, he must have a girl of his own; it would be silly if he didn't have with such a handsome face. And I'm so ugly, I said to myself, and I pretended to have something in my eye so that I could look at myself in the mirror without Cook thinking I was vain. I would

130

be thirty in a week and my first bloom had gone, I was old to get started with men. I had kept myself intact, though, and any man who claimed me would be getting all of me, I'd be his complete, as it were. I stared at my reflection in the kitchen mirror and I thought: No, Mary Longhurst, you're not so bad, you'll pass muster, worse things than you have reached the stage of raising a family.

He called—not at six on the dot, but at five minutes past. I was ready for him at the top of the basement steps. I had on my best summer outfit—a navy polka-dot print and a smart white hat and a very stylish pair of shoes which hurt me rather. He took me to the Empire, I think it was, and he placed his hand on mine some time during the main feature: it had Garbo in it, I've forgotten its name, but I know I cried (and so did George, I'm certain, I had my suspicions) because she looked so lovely. She looked so cool, too, and I felt awful, really awful, because I'd begun to sweat very badly: I reminded myself not to touch my hair when we left the cinema—if I did, he would see the stains in the pits of my arms. His hand was still in mine as we strolled through Piccadilly, I was in a daze after the film, it had captured my imagination, I wanted to stand on the prow of a ship with the wind in my hair, and he had to ask me three times—he told me afterwards—if I wanted a bite to eat.

I did, I was peckish, but I knew his income from the grocer's wasn't of the Rothschild kind, so I said no, I didn't. He pulled me to a halt and he turned me round and after kissing me he said 'You bloody liar. I could hear your stomach rumbling in the Empire.' I laughed at that and I looked at him and he was grinning. And then I stopped laughing all of a sudden because it dawned on me that I loved him. I didn't worry about caution, for once, so I gave him his kiss back and to spare. I heard 'Mary, I love you' and wondered where it had come from.

Thursday was our day for months on end, and we had some Sundays together, too. We went to Marble Arch many a fine afternoon, to the Speaker's Corner that is, and I'd never seen so many people with tempers before or heard such strong words.

Other times we went to Hampton Court, which I liked because of the history, or to Box Hill, which George said was like being in the country. I'd show him the country one day, I said, this isn't the country it's just a few trees and a bit of grass—where I came from, on spring or summer days, it was green and blue for as far as the eye could see.

It was there, one day when we were spread out, that he asked me to be his wife. He had bided his time until now, he said, because he wanted something decent to offer me by way of a home. He had ambitions. He had worked hard, often after the proper hours, and had put all his spare money to one side. There had been no girls before me to blow his wages for him. The long and the short of it was that he had seen a little property in Camberwell and had set his heart, as the saying goes, on buying it. How did I fancy running a newspaper shop with him at my side? Of course I fancied it, it was a dream come true so to speak, we'd be what they called business people in our own small way. 'Oh, George, I *do* fancy it,' I said, and we got up that very minute and took the long bus ride to Camberwell and stood in the street outside our future home like a couple of tailor's dummies, stock still and not a word on our lips. I asked myself what I had done to deserve such happiness.

He bought the shop first thing on the Monday morning, he signed the papers and sorted out all those complicated things you have to do by law when you branch out on your own. I gave in my notice and we went that same evening to the church I'd been praying at since I'd come to London and we named the day to the vicar, who was ever so nice to us. George took me to a pub, I was wary about going in, I'd never been in a proper bar before, only the Bottle and Jug part on errands for my father. Anyhow, he coaxed me in, this was a special occasion, and it was really quite pleasant inside, no drunkards or crude language, and he ordered a sherry for me and a whisky for him.

I wrote and told my parents the news and my mother came up to see me on a day trip and she looked George over in a cafeteria and I sensed that he wasn't quite what she had it in her mind for me to marry. Well, for once in my life, Mam, I said to myself, I am going to have my way, you can keep your advice to yourself for once. But all she said to me as we waited at the station for her train was 'Has he been at you, Mary?' and I said no, of course he hadn't, what could she be thinking. 'That's my good girl,' she said. 'Let him wait, it'll be worth more that way.' I asked her if she liked him. She replied that she couldn't properly tell on a first meeting but he hadn't a straight look in his eye, that was one thing for sure.

Straight look or no straight look, we were standing at the altar a fortnight later. George was an orphan so he only had his brother Victor and Victor's wife, Kitty, to represent his side as it were. My father was red in the face because of his collar being too tight, he was never the man to dress up anyway, and he said to me after the ceremony that it was all he could do to keep himself from scratching as he was giving me away due to the wool rubbing against his skin – he had one suit for all weathers, it was best for winter really, you can imagine how he must have felt wearing it in the heat.

There was neither time nor money for a honeymoon—we didn't want to go off, anyway, with our little shop waiting there for us. We had a bit of a reception, nothing grand, at some hotel rooms near by, and then we went by bus and tram to Camberwell – I had my wedding-dress, which I'd changed out of, in a suitcase with my other clothes. George carried the new Mrs Hicks over the threshold, naturally, and he called me his Camberwell beauty, which was a play on words. We had nothing to speak of yet in the way of furniture – an old crock of a table to eat off and a chair and a bed, of course, a double one, room enough for two, which we found ourselves lying in before much time had passed. We'd undressed with our backs to each other, so he was very surprised when he saw me in my nightie. 'You won't be needing that tonight,' he said. 'You've got me here to keep the wind out.'

And I have to admit I was surprised by it, I was thirty-one and starry-eyed for my age – there were girls of seventeen who knew more of life in that department. George had trouble with me, he almost lost patience – oh no, oh please no, let me stay calm and not panic, I remember I thought – and, after a while, he stopped in his tracks, so to speak, and said, 'Farmer Giles never had your drawers off in the cabbage patch, did he?' We had a laugh and got our breath back and he finally put himself into me. I bled afterwards and I managed – because it was my wedding-night and I was supposed to be happy – to steady my nerves. In the morning he was slower about it and I joined in more even though I was drowsy – I had my moment when he did, he was contented and I felt like a real woman at long, long last.

There was so much to do to the shop before it was fit for the public to see. Mr Dacre from next door spent a whole day clearing out the chimney – the Blackwall Tunnel couldn't have been grimier, it was his opinion. And the two of us – George and me, that is – washed all the surfaces and gave the shelves and the walls a fresh lick of paint. I polished the counter – with the help of a little spit and a lot of elbow grease – until it shone. Not once that week did I have to clench my fists or keep my feet firm – I was too excited, I couldn't wait for the shop to open, I was on top of the world, as the saying goes.

Then, once we were opened, once we were in business, the newspapers tidily piled and the confectionery and the few bits of stationery nicely arranged in their separate places, we wondered where on earth our customers were. I found myself being very sensible – George was letting his feelings show, he was often disheartened, he'd snap when spoken to – and it pleased me, it really did, to tell him not to be soft, he was a man of substance now, he couldn't expect miracles to happen straight away. He had to have patience, I told him. It was a change for me to have another person leaning on my shoulder.

I gave him the right advice. I won't say that people rushed to buy our papers and sweets, that would be a lie, but we began to see a few notes in our till instead of the usual small coins. The odd occasional customers became regular ones and they spread the word about us and things brightened generally and so did George.

I made friends with the neighbours — mainly because I wanted to, I like friendliness, but also because when you're in a city you have so many families on all sides of you that it doesn't pay to harbour ill-feelings or have rifts. George, who had never held himself aloof in his dealings with me through our courting days, behaved very strangely I thought when the Harroways and the Dacres and some others in the district made the effort to know us better — he kept his distance, I must say. He could be very off-hand. It was always me who kept the peace: it was his nature, I said, he'll open out with you in time, you'll see.

In the September, I think it was, I went to see Dr Pashley to ask him about the sickness I had that kept coming on — waves of it, I told him, and giddiness too. He gave me a thorough examination and said I was in a fit state and that in a few months I'd be a proud mother, if his word was anything to go by. I told George my news over our meal that evening, and he came across and lifted me up from my chair and looked me up and down and then he said he was glad he had married me.

When my Ralphie arrived — Ralph was George's idea, it had been his father's name — we were much more comfortably settled. It was more like a home above the shop. I could show visitors our living quarters with pride now. We had a small suite, nothing grand, in the best room at the front, which George called the state apartments because there seemed no end to the dusting and such that I did in it. George would lie on the sofa after a hard day and lose himself in one of his books — he was improving his mind, he said — while I sat knitting. 'You may be improving your mind, George Hicks, but you're not improving my furniture.' So I made some covers for the backs of the chairs and sofa, anti-macassars, and told George he could rest his head on them without my nagging.

Ralphie was a beautiful baby, needless to say, very docile for a boy, he'd be in his pram and you'd forget he was there. I opened my throat a bit again and sang him to sleep, as Mam had done with me. All manner of funny old songs came back to me, lullabies even. Mrs Harroway — Milly's mother, that is — told me my voice worked better than cocoa on her at bedtime.

Then the war was on us. 'If you read the papers you sold', George said, 'you wouldn't be so surprised about it.' The army asked to see him. He went off that Monday morning in his new serge suit, but he came home at five in a rage the like of which I had never seen him in. 'I'm not needed. I'm a physical wreck.' 'But you're not, George.' 'That's what they bloody told me,' he shouted. 'Go and ask them if you don't believe me.' I stayed quiet, I made him some tea, I was overjoyed but I couldn't say – he wouldn't go and be killed in a foreign country, I wouldn't have those long weeks and months of worry. It was silly of him to have so much pride, he should be thankful to have his life spared. But you can't tell a man about his pride.

Ralphie was turned three when we sent him to his grandparents. He would stay with them until the war was over. I was happy in one respect – he would have a country upbringing, the best kind there is, he'd be healthy, he'd be free to roam. He'd taste my mother's cooking. I said goodbye to him in the cottage one wet Saturday: how he cried, how he clutched at my dress! 'There, there, my Ralphie,' I said to him, 'I'll soon be down to see you.' Mam said she had a cry-baby for a grandson, a real spoilt darling – I could see, for all her remarks, that her heart had gone out to him. Nothing ever spoke truer than my mother's eyes.

George worked for the Home Guard and I ran the shop myself those times he was away. It was quite a job, it really was, especially when rationing came in. The sirens went off many evenings when he wasn't with me, and then we'd all be bundled together – the neighbours, that is – in the shelter: the Harroways, Mrs and Miss, became my closest friends during those terrible days. We cheered one another. George complained whenever he came home and saw the three of us in the scullery or the front room or elsewhere in the house. 'Bloody women and their stupid bloody chatter,' he'd say to me once they were gone. He had taken to swearing.

And he wasn't considerate any more – I put it down to the war and his pride being hurt; I had to think of a reason. Let him brood, I told myself, he'll be himself again, he'll be your George. He's under a strain. When he just satisfied himself and left me there, I still said nothing. When he came to accuse me — and I knew there would be such a day although I prayed against it — it couldn't be of nagging.

I went to see Ralphie. On the train I had a thought that sent me cold, a chill all the way up my back; I told myself off, I really did, for thinking it. It had no foundation, so to speak. If George goes from me — it was my thought — I always have my son, my Ralphie, to cling to. I suppose you might say it was a premonition, if that's the right word.

I felt lighter when I was back in Camberwell, a great deal better for having seen Ralphie so happy. He had filled out and there was colour in his cheeks. He was still wetting his bed, though, which was a cause for concern — no amount of pepper on his sheets had stopped him, my mother said. I told George his boy was thriving and growing and that he sent him a kiss. George said 'Does he?' and went off to his duties.

We lived in this way for a long time — him being distant and short-tempered, me not saying a word on the subject in case of further troubles. I put my heart and soul into the shop and the home. He would come out of his gloom one day, he would open his eyes and see how much he had to be grateful for — what comfort he had about him and the love I still had it in me to give. A war was on, and although he was a soldier at half-cock only — which is how he talked of himself — he was seeing some nasty sights for all that. He had cleared away rubble after bombings and had pulled out bodies.

And then, one Sunday, I couldn't steady myself. I was giving the front room a thorough cleaning and all of a sudden I was brought to a stop, as it were, because the dust didn't seem to be going away; I kept looking round to where I'd just cleaned and there it was, a fresh pile. I clenched my fists and told my feet to stay firm. 'Mary Hicks, it's the sunlight playing tricks with your eyes.' But it wasn't: I ran my finger along the top of the sideboard and it was thick black when I'd finished. I carried on —

a system was the answer, I told myself – but only a short while afterwards it was there again, as much of it as ever. It would never end, I couldn't cope with it, it would cover everything we owned. There was nothing I could do but cry.

˙You're as cheerful as a ghost,' he said as he lay next to me that night. 'You've moped all evening.' 'And what about you?' I caught myself asking. 'I've been treated like a brick wall, haven't I, for two years or more. What's my moping when you think of that?' I waited for his answer. I was ashamed, I had broken my vow – to be silent and patient, that is – and I even wondered if he would hit me. What with the dust, and my worries, I was being sent daft, I really was. 'Tell me what's the matter, George,' I said, as soon as I realized that he wasn't going to speak. 'You wouldn't understand, with your little mind,' he said, and he turned his back to me.

So I had a little mind, had I? I wouldn't understand, would I? What was it, I asked him, that was so beyond me I couldn't help him? 'Sleep,' he said. 'Go to sleep.' I begged with him. 'It's nothing.' I was told, in the voice you use for a child, to go to sleep. 'I can't until you tell me,' I said. It was then that I swallowed my pride, so to speak, I followed my feelings – I put my hand where he had always put it for me. He was finished with me before my moment. It was the wrong time to ask more questions.

Although I was never a one for words I wrote a lot of letters to my mother, with plenty of love and kisses for Ralphie at the bottom, of course. I didn't mention what was happening between us naturally, I just passed on news – where bombs had landed and so forth. I managed to visit once or twice but then there was a long gap, six months if I recall: Ralphie looked at me, I can see his face to this day, I might have been a Red Indian when I bent down to greet him. Mam told me off for getting into a state, I couldn't expect him to rush into my arms after six months.

'What's that husband of yours up to?' she asked me.

He was in the Home Guard still, I said.

'Is he leading you a dance as ever?'

'No, Mam,' I said and wondered what she meant. When

Ralphie had gone out to play, 'Why is he leading me a dance?' was the first thing I asked her. 'There's much I don't know in this world, Mary, and I've never made bones about it, but no one can teach me when it comes to reading between the lines in the letters my daughter sends me. What's he about?'

'I don't know.'

'You'll lose him, my girl. You're not enough for him. I've met him barely three times but I gathered that much.'

For a moment or so I felt how nice it would be, I'd have no cares, to stay there on the farm. Someone else would cope with the dust and I could watch over Ralphie, he'd grow up in my sight, as it were, he'd be more like my own son. Then I told myself to come back down to earth again: it was wicked to even think of it, the very idea of sweeping George to one side. And anyway, I wasn't going to lose him without letting him see first that I had some fight in me, I was a country girl and not a city miss, I wouldn't let him ride over me just as he pleased.

But, when I was home once more – if you could call it a home, that is – I saw all too clearly that I'd be hard put to it finding a chance to do battle with him. He was a man who hated scenes. He'd say 'Shut up' or 'It's nothing' or 'I'm reading' or 'I'm tired'. I'd watch him sometimes with his nose stuck into a library book – it was history as a rule; when there were pictures the people had funny old clothes – and I'd say to myself 'He's improving his mind.' When the war ended we were more like a neighbourhood again, with so many husbands and sons back with their families. George's brother Victor had been decorated for bravery and he and his wife Kitty drove over for Sunday tea: he was itching to get on with his work again, he said, his palms had a nasty rash on them that only a steady flow of money could cure. Once a businessman always a businessman: thanks to Jerry he had five years to catch up on. 'Are you satisfied with this little place, George?' he asked. 'It can't bring you much.' 'It brings me enough,' said George and then I laughed and said 'Yes, and I do all the work in it.' 'I'd expand if I were you,' Victor went on to say. 'I only speak for myself, George, but I'd go on from here if I were you.' 'There are more important things than making money, Victor. This is enough for me and that's that.'

Kitty, I noticed, was quite a one with her airs and graces, quite the lady, I didn't really believe her when she told me how lovely my front room was, due to the look that went with it. But I had to feel sorry for her, I must say, when we were having our women's chat over the dishes: count your blessings, Mary Hicks, I said to myself, for all your troubles you don't have a son in a lunatic asylum, you don't have the misery of knowing that you've brought a madman into the world.

It was Mrs Yelverton who told me about Laura Potter. Mrs Yelverton remembers every wedding in the district for years back and she is a pleasant woman even if she does spend half her life behind her curtains. She intended no malice, I feel sure; it came out naturally that she had seen George walking with Laura Potter, who was the new secretary to the manager at the printing works. Deep in conversation, they had been, with their heads down almost on to their chests: people were making way for them on the street because it was obvious their feet were leading them. It was a wonder they hadn't gone smack into a wall.

I handed him his lamb chop with peas and new potatoes and I asked him, calmly and with no shake in my voice, who Laura Potter was.

'Why?'

'You were seen with her.'

'I'm bloody sure I was.'

I meant nothing wrong, I said, no suggestions were being made. Was she a friend of his?

'Yes. I shall be seeing her tonight.'

He finished his meal and left his plate by the sink. He put his jacket on and went out. I looked at myself in the bedroom mirror before I lay down and wept.

The next morning he was halfway through his kipper when he said, 'We must have another bed. I can't get to sleep these nights. If I'm on my own perhaps I will drop off quicker.'

Dr Pashley, I said, would give him tablets.

'A new bed's the answer, not his bloody pills. You can choose one today while I look after the shop. I'll sleep in the old bed as I'm broader than you are.'

He'd decided; he'd got it all worked out. I went, like a lamb, and chose the bed. It was delivered that very day.

And I even crept into it when he told me to. Like a lamb, I was, doing his bidding. Where had my fight gone? He told me during the night to stop my snivelling. His voice came to me from the other side of the room.

When things are bad for you, you can always rely on them to get worse. I was cleaning the next day, having a struggle to steady myself because of the name Laura Potter coming in and out of my head all the time, when George walked in and handed me a telegram. I have always had a fear of telegrams, I only receive them when it's bad news. 'Open it,' he snapped at me. 'The boy's waiting in the shop for your reply.' I tore the envelope open and I read the message and I said to tell the boy 'On my way', that was all, 'On my way'.

My father had collapsed early that morning. I packed a case and left for the country on the five o'clock train.

We sat at his side—my mother and me, that is—until it was light. He sat up as the cock crew and then he lay back and died. My mother closed his eyes. She smoothed his hair and kissed him. It was more than her usual peck.

Ralphie was up early. We had breakfast together. He liked his school, he said, because the other children were all stupid. I told him his grandfather had gone to London. He went out to play.

'The boy's at the door,' Mam said. I looked round and there was Ralphie—he'd caught us washing my father down. I didn't want him to see a dead body so early in his life, it upset me enough and I was a grown woman, but Mam took it all in her stride and made him take a proper peep, as she said. Ralphie was very curious and asked what we were doing. 'We're making him sweet for his Maker,' Mam said.

Once the funeral was over, Mam and me agreed that it was time for Ralphie to return to his rightful home. The war was ended and there was no reason for him to stay. But would he go with me without a fuss? No, he would not. He fretted and he sulked, it surprised me the way he behaved. I sat opposite him in the train and wondered if he was my son, I really did. I tried coaxing him with sweets and fruit but it was no use, he went on sulking. Oh no, I remember I prayed, don't you be a stranger too.

'Why did you bring him back?' my husband asked from the other bed that Tuesday night.

'He's your son, George,' I reminded him.

'Wasn't he happy there?'

'I need him here, George. It's unnatural for him to grow up away from us.'

'If you say so.'

And there he stopped. He was snoring minutes later.

It was nothing to George—the boy's future, the boy's schooling. It was Laura Potter he cared about: he didn't even have to say so. When the boy sulked he said 'Shut up'—it didn't occur to him to try to make him happy. It was me who did all the pretending that we were a united family.

'You're as bad as your father for reading,' I said to Ralphie once when he was being annoying and not listening to me. 'What's bad about it?' he asked straight back, it shook me, he was only nine. 'I meant,' I said, 'it's bad to read when someone is trying to talk to you.' To which he came out with, cool as a cucumber: 'Why don't you say what you mean then?'

I told Mrs Harroway about his two remarks and she said, 'You've got a bright spark there, I'll be bound.' I was really very proud of him, I was glad to have a bright spark for a son, if he grew up to be clever he would know right from wrong, he would be respectable and clean and decent.

One evening I was in one of my states—no matter how much I tidied, the house was still in a mess from top to bottom; the joint was tough and I'd cooked the cabbage so long it had no taste left in it—when George said to Ralphie, 'Come on, Ralph boy, up you get. Let's walk.' Ralphie, who hated walking with me, he made it plain, jumped to his feet as quick as lightning. I asked them where did they think they were going off to. 'We want some peace, don't we, Ralph boy?' and Ralphie said 'Yes, Dad.' I wanted to shout: I give you all the love. Your father gives you nothing. He only has to lift his little finger to get your affection.

But I didn't speak. I was so upset, the words would have come out wrong, I wouldn't have made myself clear. I was never a one with words like my husband and my son.

That night I called to George if he was awake and when he said 'Yes' I asked him to tell me what I didn't want to know: 'Do you love her?' It was a long time before I heard 'Yes. Go to sleep.'

He started to take Ralphie out a lot – to the zoo, to museums. He was never loving to him; it was more like the master and his dog to watch them together – George giving the orders and Ralphie obeying. 'Come on, Ralph boy, out we go.' 'Yes, Dad.' 'Do you fancy a stroll, Ralph boy?' 'Yes, Dad.'

Then there was scandal in the street. Mr Harroway, who hadn't long been back from the war, packed a suitcase – people said – and left his wife. He was seen going into Mrs Herring's boarding-house near the station wearing his best suit. When I was told, I remember I thought: Ah well, Mary Hicks, you're not the only one with troubles. I didn't like to mention the subject, it would have been vulgar as well as cruel, to Milly or Charlie or even the poor victim herself: I carried on in the shop all natural, pretending that our little world was in apple-pie order.

But Mrs Harroway herself came in to tell me. I poured us both a sherry and I asked her if she knew who Laura Potter was. Yes, she did all right – she was that long one with red hair who had a reputation with men. 'I've never seen her,' I said. 'Is she pretty?' 'Well, Mary, she wears a lot of war-paint, but as to pretty –' 'You know about her and George, do you?' 'Yes, Mary, I'm afraid I do. Everybody does in these parts.' Oh my Lord, I thought, the shame of it, everybody knowing. I couldn't stop my tears although I tried to. I brought myself up short – Mrs Harroway had come to *me* for comfort, not vice versa.

'Men,' I said. 'Men.'

'Yes,' said Mrs Harroway. 'You might well say it. Men.' She came out with her story: her husband *hadn't* gone because of the widow, Mrs Herring; it was her—Mrs Harroway's—feet trouble that was to blame. 'Look how they've swelled up,' she said. Mr Harroway hated illness and he didn't like nasty blemishes on the person either—was it likely that he'd go off to a woman with an unsightly birth-mark just above her wrist? No, I replied, it wasn't likely. I sobbed and said 'George.' Ralphie walked in at that moment, I was being comforted, and seeing him there, young and innocent, made me feel all the worse. Mrs Harroway asked him if he loved me and he said 'Yes.'

It grieves me now to recall those scenes between us—George and me, that is. I had a little mind, I heard over and over. He could talk with Laura Potter, she had an interest other than her home and her housework. 'Yes,' I said. 'Stealing husbands, that's her interest.' 'Your bloody little mind,' he said. He would call me, in a voice so quiet and cold that it frightened me, Mary Longhurst. 'My name is Hicks,' I'd remind him. 'You married me. My name is Hicks.' Why didn't he live with his beautiful Laura? No, he said, he preferred things as they were.

Ralphie was eleven when George keeled over and died in front of me in the shop. I came out of my daze and felt his pulse. I shook him. I stood up. 'Oh George,' I said. He was gone now, finally gone from me. I bent down again and did to my man what my mother had done to hers: I closed his eyes and I kissed him gently, on the lips. I locked the shop door and pulled down the blind. I went back to George. I stood and looked at him; I couldn't move. It was only when I caught the smell—being dead, he had made a motion—that my legs obeyed me and I had the sense to get help.

A look that I've seen many times since came over Ralphie's face at the grave-side. He stared at the hole for his father's coffin like someone gone into a trance. It was mud rather than dust the parson sprinkled.

'There's his fancy woman walking away,' said Milly. 'She

had a nerve to come.' I had a son to live for, which was a good deal more than some poor women had, I told myself: life could be treating me worse. He shunned my affection, it was true; I reached the stage where I felt he would brush me aside if I showed him any fondness. I heard him scream once or twice, coming out of nightmares I should imagine. I nearly went to his room—I could wipe the sweat away; I could send him off to sleep again—but two thoughts stopped me: I didn't want to hear him telling me to go away; I hoped that, by going through his ordeal without me, he would become a stronger man for it.

He took to his studies with a vengeance. He burnt the midnight oil, as the saying goes. I peeped over his shoulder once to see what he was reading. It was poetry. I said to him I thought it was funny putting words on a page like that.

I tried starting conversations with him. 'Yes,' he'd say; 'No,' he'd say, or he'd grunt. I explained about Milly's operation and how the doctors were cutting in, but I might just as well have mentioned the weather: he had no interest in other people.

We went, the two of us, on a coach to Kent, which I considered really earned its title of the Garden of England: it was an August day, as hot as any I can remember, and there were so many flowers it dazzled your eyes to see them all. Ralphie hardly spoke to me—he was annoyed with me for putting my foot down and insisting that he should be smart in his person—and his nose, as usual, was in his book. But he was different once we were at the asylum, where we were paying a visit on his cousin Harry—George's brother Victor's boy, that is. He drank in the surroundings, he really did, and I swear I saw something very like pity pass across his face when he was talking to his poor cousin. That's what it pleased me to think, anyway.

It was a relief to me, though, when we were home again and in the kitchen—it was like being back in the real world, so to speak. He told me to shut up, I was talking too much, the trip had upset him. He began to cry—the first tears I'd seen him shed since he was a child. At last, I thought, at long, long last. The tears over, he spelt his name out—an R and an A and an L and a P and an H — in the same way that his cousin had done, and this caused us to laugh. I went to bed that night a happy woman, lighter in my heart, although my gums were sore from the new teeth which Mr Cottie had fitted me with.

Hours later his scream woke me. I got as far as his door and then I stopped to listen. Don't fuss, Mary Hicks, he'll only accuse you of fussing. Keep the peace.

I watched him as he thrived and grew. At the school the masters told me they wished all their pupils were as sharp and as willing to learn as Ralphie — they'd have no problems then. I have to admit I preened myself at the prize-givings: Ralph Hicks, it was, Ralph Hicks; you heard the name throughout the evening.

Even so, for all his cleverness, it wasn't like having a son about the house. 'Study me,' I wanted to say many a time, 'study *me*.' But did I say it? No, I didn't. He hated scenes as much as his father had, it hurt me the more to see him so collected, I should have been allowed to share his joys and sorrows. When I *did* try to argue him out of himself he simply went walking.

The neighbours started to drop like flies, they really did. Mrs Yelverton wondered if we'd have a street left, the rate they were going: first Mr Dacre from his collapsed lungs; then Mr Harroway in his sleep at the boarding-house, the second man to everyone's knowledge — there might have been more — that the widow had laid low; Mr Poole himself, young for his age, who was given the best send-off in living memory, by his own firm of course — it was as bad as the cholera that her grandmother had told her about. Then my good friend Mrs Harroway went, poor Grace, and I missed her dearly. Then my own mother — though not in Camberwell, in the country, I was rung up with the news. I never expected that Ralphie would refuse to come with me — to her funeral, that is. But he did. I told him it was his own flesh and blood they were putting in the earth. I reminded him how he'd been happy when he'd stayed there, he'd loved his time on the farm. And I even said how worried I had been once that he would grow up closer to his grandmother than he was to me.

I mentioned his father, too – mentioning his father sometimes made him think – but it was no use. I buried my mother by myself as it were and I am sure the people in the village had something to say on the matter. Anyway, that's all the past: death isn't a subject I wish to linger over. It comes to us all is my opinion.

I shiver at the thought of what would have become of me without Milly, who has been both a boon and a comfort. I had always felt for her, even before we became close friends. It is a terrible thing in this life of ours that certain people should be made to suffer so much while others have no pain or troubles at all. But there it is, it's the way the Lord wills it, He must have some purpose up His sleeve. Milly, her mother once told me, had had more than her fair share of childhood illnesses, so it was nothing less than a cruel blow when she was struck by her Parkinson's in the prime of her life. It was touch and go at the hospital, it really was, because of the operation being such a delicate one. To this day she has a bald patch in the middle of her head, which she will always have, and every now and then her shakes come on, but at least she functions, she is not the vegetable she might have been without the benefit.

She has kept me together, so to speak, Milly has, all of one piece. These days there is a kind of love between us, by which I mean nothing dirty. Without her, as I say, it doesn't bear thinking, I might not have lasted, I might well have gone under. She helped me in the shop – she was often sharp with the customers, I must say, but then some of them deserved a good talking-to – and when Ralphie wasted his education by taking on ridiculous jobs and not caring what became of him, she was there to calm me, firm as a rock.

He broke what was left of my heart by his attitude. I had pinned my hopes on his becoming someone, a person of importance, it would make amends. It pained me not to know what he was going to do. He had learnt so much and now he was wasting it. His masters wanted him to go to university – but did that suit his lordship? No, it did not. I told him he made no sense to me, none at all. And when he asked 'Why not?' I all but screamed back that I wished to God I knew. He seemed to delight in ruining his chances, his eyes lit up, it was as if all he'd achieved with his books had been in vain. I pleaded with him for his father's sake not to be a fool.

But, as with everything else, it was no use. He got his way, he did what he wanted. He washed dishes in a restaurant and he worked on a building site, of all shameful things. He went to the printing works, too. Then he came home one evening and ate his meal with us in his usual way and after he'd wiped his mouth on his napkin he said, 'I shall be a teacher, I think.' 'Is that what you want?' I asked him. 'It will pass the time. I might as well do something with all the useless information I carry about with me.' It was Milly who remarked, when he'd gone out, that it was a funny reason for taking up teaching and no mistake. Still, it was better, all things considered, than having to put up with the shame of having a son who was occupied like a common labourer.

He went off to his college to train and during the time he was away I decided to sell the shop; Milly and me decided between us, that is. We would wait until Ralphie was back, I said, and had started in his new job before we did what was necessary to dispose of the property. 'Why wait for him? Why consider him? He's never in his life considered you' were Milly's words. She was right, of course, Milly *is* right about most things. 'Even so,' I said to her.

Ralphie caused no trouble, for once. 'I was going anyway,' he said. 'I could do with some peace.' So he took himself off across the river with his father's bed and his shelves of books, and I saw and heard little more of him for months after. He moved and so did we—into the flat which I bought with the money, not much but enough, that I got for the shop. It is a small flat but we are snug in it. It will become Milly's one day, if I have the good fortune to die first.

He brought his future wife to see us. I was surprised I must admit, he'd never had a girl friend as a boy. Come to that, he'd had no friends of any description—except, that is, for Laura Potter, whom it reached my ears he'd visited every so often. Dr Pashley said he was the most unusual child he had ever seen—I can see the truth in his words now, though I was hurt at the time.

There she stood, Elspeth Chivers. 'Call me Ellie,' she said in a friendly fashion. I told her how clever my Ralphie had been and she listened to me and smiled. I was not sure that I liked her: it was something about her manner, she cast the sort of looks at me that you only give to children when they're sick. 'An eager miss,' said Milly. '*Too* eager for him.' And there was her better birth, as well—it stuck out. 'Well,' was all I could think of to say in reply, 'if she's the one he wants I wish him joy of her.'

We were both invited, naturally, to his wedding. Oh, it was such a dark and dismal place, that office, it smelt so, and you could hear people shouting from inside the swimming baths next door. I missed the white, I told him, and I said I hoped they would think again and have a church wedding later on to compensate, as so many other couples did these days. Sometimes, when George upset me, I would think back to my lovely wedding and it gave me consolation to recall the white and all the ceremony. Ralphie took his bride off to a foreign country for a short honeymoon, and I smiled to myself and thought, 'They won't be as happy on theirs as we were on ours—the honeymoon that never was.'

I wrote to him when Laura Potter died, I called him Ralph in the letter, 'Ralphie' didn't seem natural to me any more. And I called her Miss Potter because that was how he always referred to her. I was sorry, I said, which was the truth. Cancer is a wicked thing for anyone to be taken out of this world by.

I wrote to him a short while ago, inviting him to come and visit, despite the fact that I am in poor health. The dreadful news about his wife had been passed on to us by Mr Proctor, the man who had looked after the arrangements for their wedding reception—Ralph's and hers, that is. He came on a Sunday and he ate with us and my heart was in my throat to help him but the words would not come out. It was funny, it was plain to me the misery he was in, but not even 'Ralphie' would come to my lips.

'He's upset you, hasn't he?' Milly said.

'Yes, Milly.'

'I shall write to him. I'm thinking of your health.'

'No, Milly,' I said. 'Don't write.'

'It's the wisest policy, Mary. In the long run.'

Milly is more sensible than me. Her feelings don't sway her like mine do. She's strong, in spite of all the complaints she's suffered. My welfare is her first concern. She says that my son has no right to make me unhappy. There is a kind of love between us, as I say. We are happy as sandpipers most of the time, the two of us. It hurts her, I know, to find me so contrary: but then my name *is* Mary, and blood *is* thicker than water, unfortunately. Milly has been kind to me and Ralphie hasn't, but the love I bear my son has deeper roots: roots I would much rather sever, I must admit, it stands to reason. Perhaps, in the next world, the good Lord will see to it that I love the correct people.

I wait for the street door to slam before I lift myself up from the floor. I look down at the remains of his screen.

The words come out easily. 'Ralph. I would rather be dead than live with your contempt. I am sick with love of you. Elspeth.'

I shall lock myself in the bathroom. I shall hack, hack, hack.

5

I write down

ME

—the word that reminds me who I am. I am Ralph Hicks, I am Mummy's Ralphie. I am not Bernard Proctor, I am not my mother, I am not my wife.
I am

HERE

in a room that overlooks a lawn surrounded by trees. It is May and the sun is shining. It is warm.

I was brought to this place, I was led along corridors, I was undressed and put to sleep.

I awoke one morning and walked in the grounds. I stood beneath an apple tree and looked up at its blossom. My mind was empty.

A shower sent me in again. I sat down. I told the nurse who came in with a poached egg and coffee that I wanted a pen and paper; I wanted those above all things.

The doctor handed me an exercise book. I opened it. Line after line; page upon empty page.

'Which?' asked the doctor. Like a conjurer, his hands were suddenly filled with pens.

Green or blue or red or brown – it was of no importance to me. Something with which to form words. I took a red one.

He left me alone.

I could not begin. Hours passed. Sick with defeat, I lay down on the bed. The lines still beckoned. They ran before me when I closed my eyes.

They became pebbles, they became blood, they became the blue light I sat under. They became the roses that turned to blood again and in which I drowned. Then they became the blossom I had looked at

EARLY

that morning, and my way was clear. Early, Early: I would write the word down and begin. 'Early' meant walking in the grounds, my head empty, the apple tree white and pink. I would find other words to lead me out of darkness. A word like – for instance –

HER

would bring Ellie to me. What was left of her. Little bits and pieces – I had to be sharp, my mind quick and my ears alert, to catch her: Elspeth Hicks, née Chivers, the daughter of a Major and his Mrs, who ended as a mess on the floor of Mrs Ruby Dinsdale's bathroom. Mrs Ruby Dinsdale is the daughter of Mrs Goacher, whom I think of as

WARM

because I could hide behind her. In her presence I was content to be nothing: a machine only, nodding and listening. Mrs Goacher was complete, she had no doubts, she was there. I sat before her and marvelled. Her view of the world was as simple as any visionary's: it was a place in which her daughter misbehaved.

She was wearing clean undergarments on the day she died, so the doctor who looked for the cause had no grounds for complaint.

With the aid of

BOY

I would run again, my arms out like wings. At the zoo three gibbons would leap into the air and a rhino would sleep on its side, unaware of the flies buzzing around its head. A carnivorous sparrow would peck at the lion's meat.

And I would scream from the top of the oak tree. In the farm later, having been rescued with ladders, I would cry from shame.

And I would clutch my father's hand and walk at his side – his shadow merging into mine, mine into his – and I would think of the

BLACK

clothes I wore at his funeral and the black sky above and the blackness of the hole he was lowered into.

Pebbles would wake me, dazzling white ...

In a state almost like excitement I left the bed. I sat down at the table and opened the book once more. I picked up the red pen and waited until my writing hand was steady.

Three weeks have gone by and I am still

HERE

in this room in this large country house with this tranquil view that too often distracts me from my purpose.

My purpose is to put them together again, these pieces of Humpty Dumpty at the bottom of the wall.

I write down a

PLEA

—to the someone, perhaps, whom I find myself talking to—that I may, slowly but certainly, creep out into the light.

But it is

HER

—she, Ellie—I must try, even now, to understand.

For I could not bear to speak in her voice. Her words would not enter my head.

And yet she told me much about herself. Her childhood in India: the tea-parties—the voices of the officers' wives, heard from the end of a long cool hall, forming themselves into one sound, a bray, as high and piercing as a trumpet note. She remembered, as well, the bundles by the river—human bundles, waiting to die. And how, years later, she returned from lunch with Mummy and saw those bundles and heard that bray and went to the lavatory and was violently ill—she had drunk too much hock, but to her it had seemed almost symbolic, a spilling-out of old ways and old habits. That day, she said, she descended the staircase of the house in Bournemouth with a great need for a new life strong inside her. The time had come to be of use.

I wake her gently and I enter without assistance. I look into her vast eyes. I say 'Cow's eyes' and she laughs: 'What a term of endearment!' We kiss.

It was my only term of endearment.

Oh God, she said once as we rested beside each other sharing a cigarette, what a change, what a blessed change it was for her to be lying next to a man she loved. A man she wanted to know more—much, much more—about. What she meant was, before she'd decided to teach, she had been a lady of the easiest virtue. In a pub one night she had heard herself referred to as 'a good lay' by a smart young stockbroker—it had not been a pleasant experience. An object, nothing more than an object, that was Ellie Chivers—a thing you laid.

But that was the past, and better forgotten. It was kaput, it was finito. It was all part of that dreadful, ghastly previous existence. The future alone was what mattered, her future with

ME

—the distant Mr Hicks, the really rather forbidding Mr Hicks, the one master the children feared.

Ellie Chivers, forgive Mr Hicks for what he brought you to.

AFTER

what he brought you to, Mrs Ruby Dinsdale—an object on a

divan, sweating and groaning – asked him to leave his long room (Our love-nest, Ellie, our palace) at his earliest convenience.

Which he did. He wandered until he found a suitable place. Mr Basil – his hair pomaded and his skin cologned – apologized for the excruciating wallpaper. He would have it changed as soon as the room became vacant again.

'Deary me,' he said one evening. 'You're not crying, are you?'

'No.'

'Conjunctivitis, could it be?'

'No. No.'

'Your eyes are very swollen, very puffy. I have some drops I can give you.'

'Thank you.'

'They're in my medicine box. Wait a moment.'

Mr Hicks waited, even though he wanted no other company but the excruciating old roses.

'Are you sure you're not crying?'

'Yes.'

'You probably need to sleep.'

'Yes.'

And yes, and yes, and yes, and yes to all the remedies suggested.

Mrs Schneider called at eleven. Would Mr Hicks lie on the rubber sheet provided? Again yes.

Mrs Schneider massaged every part of him. 'Into the shower with you, there's a good boy' were the only words she spoke.

Mr Basil said it had been a first-rate show. Mr Hicks could forget the week's rent as a token of gratitude.

In the street outside, in the chill night air, Mr Hicks did not bother to use his fists as windscreen-wipers. Let them flow, let the bloody things flow. No sorrow, no reason. Let them flow until their springs were dry.

Suddenly Mr Hicks saw himself as he had been

THEN

and he remembered the fear that had choked him as the army entered his classroom and how he had opened his throat as wide as was humanly possible and the sound that was more like a howl than a scream had miraculously escaped.

It was over. Everything quiet. Mr Basil on his doorstep like a figure on a frieze.

'Go and rest, Mr Hicks. Have a good long sleep. I shall call my doctor in the morning.'

And now Mr Hicks is

HERE

among his fellow ruins, the ones for whom little is humanly possible. Mr Hicks—alias Mummy's Ralphie, alias

ME

is oh such a familiar specimen. You know him well. You see him daily. He should carry a bell, as lepers do—smell me, lick my wounds, hear my screams. I am an Alienated Man, you know me well, I am oh such a familiar specimen. There is a wall too near me. I beat my head against it and I crumble to pieces. I watch it happen with my glassy eyes. I cannot see beyond myself.

I am trying, though. I am trying, at last, to look out. With the aid of words. A word like—for instance—

and Master Hicks – each hair on his head beautifully in place; his face scrubbed to a shine – is listening to his fat mad cousin as he spells his name out. He looks at Harry and feels something very like pity. Or is it the thought that, argy-bargy, Ralphie is Harry and Harry Ralphie?

Nothing in this bloody world makes sense to Master Ralphie. He stares like a fool at a fool who can outstare him.

Later, in the kitchen, among the reassuring properties of every-day life – pots and pans and jars, and cups hanging in rows along the dresser – he finds release. He weeps. His mother comforts him. She strokes his hair. 'There, there,' she says. 'Men don't cry, Ralphie.'

But they do, Mother. Men do. That is the opinion of fully-grown Mr Hicks who writes down

WARM

because the pain he feels now for not having felt pain then – her pain, his pain, their pain; the pain, the pain, the pain that thrives and grows, that expands, that unites the truly living – is too much for this pitiful wreck with his cheap self-loathing and his cheaper despair.

He writes down

WARM

once more, he hopes for the last time. He sees Mrs Goacher, and his wife, Ellie, and Bernard, their friend. It is the day of Mrs Goacher's Command Performance. An appreciative audience –

in the form of Mr Hicks *and* Mr Proctor—ensures that every piece in the Goacher repertoire will be played.

She begins:

'Christ, Mr Hicks dear, those stairs will be the death of me.'

'Mrs Goacher, meet a friend of ours—Bernard Proctor.'

'Charmed, I'm sure. You're not religious, are you?'

'No, not in the least.'

'That's good to hear. Not that I've anything against believers—except the one, that is. Me saying "Christ" didn't offend you, did it?'

'No, Mrs Goacher, not at all.'

'I hate to offend, I really do. In my view, there are too many people giving offence these days. But then, I was brought up to respect manners, unlike some—I come from a time when there were still a few ladies and gentlemen left, the type you could look up to. Stop me if I'm droning on. How's the nice Mrs Hicks today? Well—are we?'

'Yes, thank you. We're well.'

'I'm glad, dear. I only wish I could say the same for this old bag of bones I carry about with me: it's far from well, I can tell you, what with bronchial trouble and a bloody great pimple in a place I wouldn't care to mention. You have to pardon my French, Mrs Hicks, I'm a vulgar old soul in many ways. Vulgar, yes, but not plain filthy, I hope.'

I invite Mrs Goacher to sit down. She nods to me and smiles at Bernard: 'I thought he'd never ask. You looked after their wedding, didn't you?—What do you do for your bread and butter, Mr Poulter?'

'Proctor, Mrs Goacher. I teach.'

'Proctor, did you say? You teach, do you? Like the young ones here?'

'Yes. I teach in the East End.'

'Ah, the East End. Salt of the earth, those people, though it *has* been said before. Them two words take me back, Mr Proctor—there, I got you right; I'm not as thick as my Ruby maintains—they take me back and that's putting it mildly.'

'Gin, Mrs Goacher?'

'Have I ever refused, Mr Hicks dear? When I say no to a gin, Her Majesty will be doing knees-up at the Follies.'

We laugh.

'And *that* really will be the day. A drop of hot water with it, Mr Hicks dear, same as my old mother used to have. You're very nicely spoken, Mr Proctor.'

'Am I?'

'Yes. Yes, you are. You're class, aren't you? You don't have to answer, I *know*. Did you ever meet the Honourable Gerald Lord?'

'No.'

'Oh, a gentleman, a man among men he was. You and he would have taken to one another.'

'Would we?'

'Oh yes. Oh yes, definitely. I could have spit when he was put away. He had peculiar tastes, if you see what I mean, he went for his own. It's a complaint, in my experience, that a lot of gentlemen are prone to. But he was no worse than my daughter in what he did, and a damned sight less greedy, I wouldn't mind betting. It's all dirty as far as I'm concerned: if you think about it, an arse is just another hole — isn't it? — and it's in just as nasty a position as the thing we women have to cope with. That side of a person's life is only nature, it's something that takes over and goes away, that's what I think. With Ruby Dinsdale, though, it's like a disease.'

Mrs Goacher looks at each of us in turn. She waits for someone to ask the right question. It is Bernard who does so: 'Why is it like a disease?'

'It's her appetite, Mr Proctor. She eats men, she honestly does. I have to speak the truth, even though she *is* my own flesh and blood. If you put all the cocks she's ever had end to end, there'd be enough of them to fit a handrail around the world.'

We laugh, Bernard and I.

'Forgive my turn of phrase, Mrs Hicks, I mean no harm. I tell you no lies, rest assured.' She smiles at Bernard. 'I won't go into details concerning Ruby, since we have a lady present —'

'The lady can always leave the room—'

'No, no, no, Mrs Hicks. Really, no. I'd be the last to drive you out of house and home. I wouldn't dream of it. No, me and Mr Proctor here—I keep getting your name right, don't I?—me and him will have a little get-together some time, the two of us, all cosy, won't we?'

'Please, Mrs Goacher, the details,' Bernard insists. 'Don't spare us.' He says that he is certain Mrs Hicks won't disapprove.

'Dare I believe him, Mrs Hicks?'

'Go ahead. Entertain them.'

'As I say, I hate to offend—'

'Amuse them, Mrs Goacher. Go ahead.'

'Right you are then.' And she launches into her aria: Ruby as an innocent child, her father's pride and joy; Ruby as a buxom schoolgirl—never a bust like it on one so young; Ruby at work, knowing her stuff when it came to shorthand and typing. And then the married Ruby, wife to Mr Dinsdale, who had a Hitler moustache and wasn't God's gift to women. Tit—of all kinds, not just Ruby's—was Ernest Dinsdale's downfall. We laugh, Bernard and I. Inspired, she continues: Ruby the stuck-up bitch, the snob, the landlady with her airs and graces and, finally, Ruby the inspector of her lodgers' light bulbs. We hear about Oswald Lavers, man of God and prophet of doom, and how he crossed himself and how he accused her—*her*, mind you—of being responsible for Ruby's ways, even down to the exposing of her naked winker, begging Mrs Hicks's pardon. We laugh, Bernard and I.

Three gins and several stories later, Mrs Goacher goes. Bernard says 'Oh, I approve of her. She's quite divine.'

We hear her breathing with difficulty as she descends the stairs.

'I think she's a terrible old freak.'

'Ellie dear, where's your charity? I'm surprised at you.'

Ellie explains. 'I'm sorry, Bernard, and I'm sorry, Ralph, but I think she's a monster. The way she talks about her daughter fills me with disgust. Ruby deserves her mother's pity, not her contempt.'

'Really, Ellie, you can't be so serious.'

163

'I'm afraid I can. I can't help it ...'
She could not help it. It was

HER

way to be serious. In earnest. The photographs on the wall—
eyes bursting, stomach distended, old body numb with grief. And
her purpose, too—to be of use, to inspire. To surround with love.
Not only them, the children, but

ME

as well. Have me, Ralph. Take me, Ralph. Her cure for every ill.
Or: Fuck me, Ralph, because even she—

HER

—Ellie—wanted to become an object. Hurt me, she said once. It
could have meant: Humiliate me, I want to be made nothing, to
walk about as you do, in the ranks of death, down among the
dead men, Ralph.

Only once, that 'Hurt me'. In a quiet, weary voice. It was
Easter. She'd returned—knapsack tied about her shoulders, hair
matted, face grubby—after four days of marching.

I had bought a screen the previous Saturday. I had seen it in a
shop and had paid the three pounds for it automatically, without
thinking. I was behind it, reading, when she entered.

'Where are you?'
'Here.'
'Where, Ralph?'

I appeared. 'I was behind this antique,' I said.

'What is it?'

'What does it look like?'

'It's a screen.'

'That's right. Clever Ellie.'

'But why?'

'What do you mean?'

'What I mean is, Ralph: why did you buy it?'

I didn't know. It had been an impulse: I saw it, I bought it. I said, 'I liked it. It appealed to me. If you move nearer you can see the design on it. It's St George fighting the dragon.'

She moved nearer. She touched it—her hand came forward, brushed against it. But then she withdrew her hand—quickly, decisively—as though afraid that the screen would bite it off.

'Ralph.' She smiled. 'You fool.'

'Am I?'

'Yes. Yes, you are.'

She kissed me.

'I've missed you.'

'Among all those people?'

'Yes.'

'You surprise me, Ellie. Saviours of the world don't usually miss their husbands.'

'Have me, Ralph. I want you to.'

'If you take a bath, I might.'

She took a bath.

'Hurt me, Ralph,' she said in a quiet, weary voice. I suppose I hurt her.

She got up. She stood by the screen. 'You fool,' she said. 'Am I so much in your way?'

'Not at all. Nothing personal.'

But it was. I had no refuge.

'You fool,' she said, yet again, and then I fell asleep.

Now I write down

because I want to see my father. I walk alongside him; our shadows merge. He is tall. My mother is in the house: we can hear the plates clanging together as she clears the table. She is in one of her states. We are happy, we have walked away from her, preferring the peace outside. It is a summer evening.

He is tall, yes. What else? The facts, the facts. Age: fifty-eight or fifty-nine – late fifties, thereabouts. Hair: black, streaked with grey. Eyes: blue.

Pebbles fall, covering him.

My monster, my comforting grotesque, my Mrs Goacher is clearer to me. I can bring her back, I can set her down, she is all of a piece. Not him, though.

And Miss Potter is clearer, the traitorous Miss Potter. I stand on the landing outside her flat. I press the bell. I wait. I knock on the door and I press the bell again. She *has* to be in. I have news to give her: I shall soon be leaving school, I shall go on to university, I shall learn, learn, learn …

The door opens. A man – in his late fifties, I think, or thereabouts – looks at me, bemused. He wears Miss Potter's green-and-gold dressing-gown: he looks absurd for it hardly covers his groin. I hear her voice – 'Is it the Hicks boy?' 'Are you the Hicks boy?' he asks. 'Yes, I am.' 'If it is, ask him to call tomorrow at seven.' 'Call tomorrow at seven, will you?' The door slams shut.

But not him. Only the

BLACK

day comes back with any clarity. Yet even here I am not alone with him any more, as I was in so many memories. Now, so long after, other people intrude: Mrs Harroway, Mr Poole, and all the guests drinking sherry or port or brandy and eating sandwiches in our best front room. There is even laughter, because Charlie Harroway is telling Billy Booth a dirty joke.

I think back to the day at the zoo. I concentrate. What do I remember? I remember the bloody animals—gibbons, rhinos, lions. And a monkey licking his tail. No, he wasn't *there*. He was on the beach.

When I write down

BOY

in the hope of seeing him, she comes to life for me, as she was. She somehow insists. Ralphie, do this and Ralphie, do that. I keep away from her as much as I can. I go for long walks, to Miss Potter, to a film. If there is no escape and I *have* to go out with her I shuffle some paces behind. She tells me to pick my feet up.

I am left with nothing but my loss of him.

I think I want to function among the living. I want to forget my loss. I want to eradicate even that.

I want to be free of him. If I don't stand up

HERE

I never will. Look, Father, I've forgotten you. You're forgotten. I dip my hands into your muddy grave and I pull out my bleeding heart. I put it back where it belongs.

It is now in its rightful place. It lives and beats.

I am

ME

—I am Ralph Hicks. I am not Bernard Proctor, I am not my wife, I am not my mother. I am no one else. And I am more than you would want me to be, my ally that was, my enemy that is, my father.

6

The bus that was taking me into enemy territory stopped at Victoria for a change of drivers. I saw through the window a display of surgical appliances, all a dull pink. One woman remarked to another that it was always the same, you never got a through run, this route was usually manned by blacks on Sundays.

(Ellie is ash now. The Major saluted me.)

The bus set off again. It crept towards Camberwell. The women cursed: what a country, what a state of affairs.

(And I have a new room in a new house in a new part of London. I shall be there again this evening, among the old roses, under a blue light.)

Someone reminded me that I had asked for Camberwell Green. I mouthed 'Thank you' and left the bus. I walked.

(Mrs Ruby Dinsdale had felt no love for Mr Ernest Dinsdale. Not the kind of love that Mrs Goacher had for Mr Goacher and he for her. Mrs Goacher in love? Those rolls of fat, that cough, those bandaged legs? If plants and stones detest, then Mrs Goacher loves.)

It was an April day and there was lilac in the Gardens.

(Bernard said she was the type and so did Mrs Chivers. Her own mother said so. A born martyr. A great dumb thing. And yet, and yet — she had more reason to live. She loved. She could teach. I could do neither. I wanted my world brightened, like some hopeless romantic. And I stood in front of the children and screamed. Howled.)

A dog licked my hand as I waited to cross the road.

(She most certainly hadn't believed me when I had given her

the reason. Me despairing of ever teaching them anything of any value? What nonsense. I had never been involved enough to feel despair. She had been discreet: 'I feel desperate', she had said, 'quite often.' She had hoped that I would tell her the truth in the future.)

I climbed the hill.

(She smothered me, that's what she did, she pulled me down. Pity and sympathy: I was one with the Negroes, the queers, the maimed. She would help me discover myself. My heart wasn't in what I did — why didn't I write? I had a way with words. I like what I do, I said, it passes my time.)

I stopped for a rest because the climb was tiring me.

(I have to hate her. I can survive if I hate her strongly enough. Enough, enough — my word. Love enough, feel enough. And now hate enough. Waking early and seeing her mess by the bed — young ladies from good families are always sluts — was when I hated her most. The floor littered with her underwear.)

I would have a drink, I decided, before I faced the enemy.

(But that was only because I was an ordered creature. I am, I still am. Tidy and clean and ordered. I have a system. True, she had made everything shine — but after that, the chaos!)

I ordered a whisky. I placed an arm on the counter but removed it when I sensed that my shirt-cuff was wet.

(And how typical that she should die as she did. Nothing subtle about a bathroom stained with blood. Perhaps the way we die is as much an indication of character as the way we talk.)

I drank.

('She knew what she was doing,' said the coroner. The hairs hanging from his nose were something to look at. Most people cut their wrists and then only as a signal of distress. They usually survived.)

I ordered another whisky. I lit a cigarette.

(Hate is better than indifference. Her mind was as little as my mother's. She had a cure for every ill. If I think about her hard enough — enough, enough — I shall soon be able to curse her. May she rot —)

I drank.

(She can't. She's ash.)

It was windy at the top of the hill. A leaf slapped against my cheek. I buttoned up my jacket to stop it flapping about me.

(No one accused me. No one said 'You killed her.' I was a cunt and a fucking cold fish for one day only. I had been pardoned.)

Rain started. I walked on. An April shower.

(Ellie the captain, Ralph the mate, Death to follow at a later date.)

I looked up at Miss Potter's window. My freedom. Someone else, I saw, collected plants.

(If I had not been flattered, if I had not told her about myself, if I had not imagined I would grow into love – if I had not done all those things I would not be chained now. My long room would be as it was before.)

Loud voices praised Him in the Tabernacle.

(I could salvage something from the wreck: I would not hear her asking 'Why?' again. Why, Ralph? Ralph, why? Mouth open, cow's eyes staring. I do not know why. Why are my eyes grey? Why is my body hairy? I had no reason to marry you. Why did you hack, Ellie? You have told me why.)

Mildred Harroway opened the door. 'It's you,' she said. 'You had better come in.'

(She has told me why. Sick with love of me. My contempt. She has won. Look at what she has made me –)

'What are you staring at?'

'Nothing.'

'Are you coming in?'

'Yes.'

I went in. She closed the door behind me.

'Weather's changeable.'

'Yes.'

(She has won. I cannot escape the sight of her. She has me drowning in the blood she shed.)

'Did you come to see your mother or to look at the coat-rack?'

'To see my –'

'Move then.'

We went into the sitting-room.

'Hullo, Mother.'

'Hullo, Ralph.'

(Ralph.)

'How are you?'

'Oh, you know, as well as can be expected. I'm not too bad, I could be worse.'

'Her back has been giving her great pain,' said Mildred.

'Now, Milly –'

'Yes, it has, Mary.'

'I'm sorry, Mother.'

'Thank you.'

(Everything neat and tidy. Mildred Harroway has a system. No dust here.)

'We have a few chairs, in case you hadn't noticed.'

'Yes.'

'Milly was being funny, having a little joke.'

'Yes.'

I sat down.

'Put your head back if you want to. The chair has a cover on it. An antimacassar.'

'Yes.'

I put my head back.

(The Major saluted from the end of the avenue. Defiance, survival. Absurd.)

'Would you like a drink?'

'A drink?'

'That's what your mother said.'

'Yes. Please.'

'We only really keep old maids' drinks, don't we, Milly? Sherry and such.'

I asked if they had any whisky.

'No,' Mildred said firmly.

'Isn't there a drop in the medicine chest?'

'No. All gone.'

'Not even a little — ?'

'No, Mary. All gone.'

'I'll have a sherry.'

'Shall we join him, Milly?'

'Yes. I don't see why not.'

Mildred Harroway poured the drinks.

'I had great trouble finding out where you were, Ralph.'

(Ralph. Ralph.)

'Had you?'

'Yes. That woman who owned your house, that common one —'

'Mrs Dinsdale?'

'Yes. She said she had no idea where you were. She was ever so abrupt, Milly said, on the phone. Even curt.'

'Was she?'

'She was,' Mildred said as she placed the sherry at my side.

'So I got Milly to ring up that Mr Proctor. He gave us his number when he wrote and told us the news. Your news, Ralph, that is.'

'And Mr Proctor knew where you were.'

'Yes. I met him. I told him.'

(His name is Mr Basil, Bernard. Let me get you a brandy, Ralph. He is called Mr Basil, Bernard. He shot down a German plane. Yes, I will have another brandy, Bernard. Yes, cremated, it's all over. You should meet Mr B — Mr Basil — he would appeal to your sense of humour. I would like to, Ralph. I'll arrange it, Bernard.)

'Your mother said "Cheers".'

'Yes. Cheers.'

'He's very polite — Mr Proctor.'

'Yes.'

'He's respectful,' said Mildred.

(Bernard, who loves Dickens, had described Mildred Harroway as looking very much like one of The Inimitable's injured women. Rosa Dartle to the life. She only needed a scar.)

'He was very considerate, he made us feel at home that is, the day you – When you married. He stopped us from feeling out of place.'

'He certainly did. Those other snobs. That mother of hers and that aunt. If she told us once that she was named after Queen Alexandra she told us a dozen times. And then that other pair, those two common women.'

'The young people were nice.'

'I only liked him.'

'Milly's very particular about people, if you remember.'

'You have to be.'

'Yes, Milly.'

'It's a lesson I've learnt.'

'You had a black man at your wedding, didn't you, Ralph?'

'Yes.'

'There's a lot of them around here.'

'Are there?'

'Yes. Little Jamaica. That's Milly's name for Camberwell now.'

'That's right. Little Jamaica.'

'Not that we disapprove, that is. It's just that there's so many.'

'Yes, Mother.'

We sat in silence.

'This won't get the joint carved,' Mildred said eventually.

Old habits die hard. 'Can I help?' I asked.

'No.'

'Trespassers will be prosecuted. That's Milly's motto where the kitchen is concerned.'

'Oh, yes.'

'The meal won't be long. The table's all laid.'

'Thank you, Milly. Give Ralph another sherry – will you? – before you go.'

Mildred looked at me. 'He has hands.' She went out. I poured myself a sherry.

'At this time of the year I start thinking about the country, Ralph.'

(Ralph. Ralph.)

'Do you?'

'Yes, I do. Yesterday, it sounds daft, I was sat here, in this very chair that is, and I must have dozed, I really must have, because I swear I thought I was on the farm again. You're not to laugh at me, I know it does sound daft, it really must, but I smelt your grandmother's hands.'

'Did you?'

'Yes.' She smiled. 'I honestly did smell them.'

(Sweet for his Maker, lad. Sweet for his Maker. There aren't many tricks you can get up to with soap and water.)

'Can you believe it?'

'Yes, Mother.'

(No sweetness for Miss Elspeth Chivers. No soap and water for her.)

'You were happy on the farm, I recall.'

'Yes, I was.'

'Happy as a sandpiper.'

(Oh Lord, to be yearning for childhood. To have reached such a state, the two of us ... I want to run now with my arms out like wings.)

'We're having roast beef with horse-radish sauce. You'll enjoy Milly's cooking. I always used to panic so over the stove.'

(Come on, Ralph boy, out we go. There's more peace to be found in the street when she's like she is tonight.)

'I got into such states, didn't I?'

'Yes.'

'I thought you'd say "Yes." I can't deny it, it's the truth.'

'Yes.'

'The cat *has* got your tongue today.'

'Yes, Mother.'

She smiled at me.

Something to say, a topic for conversation: 'Can I pour you another glass of sherry?' was the best that Ralph Hicks, man of words, could manage.

'Oh no, thank you. I've never had a head for drink.'

'No.'

'It would make me giddy.'

Mildred called to us to sit at table. We did so. She brought in the food.

'The vegetables are all English, Ralph. Nothing foreign.'

We ate in silence.

'You haven't lost your appetite.'

'No, Mother.'

'There's treacle pudding to follow,' Mildred said.

'Ralph used to be a demon for his grandmother's gooseberry tart.'

'Was he, Mary?'

'Yes, Milly.'

'Does he want a piece of my treacle pudding?'

'Yes. Please.'

(Eating was something to do. No words. Jaws working.)

Mildred said 'What are you going to do with yourself?'

'Me?'

'I'm not looking at anyone else.'

'I haven't thought.'

'You should.'

'Give him time, Milly.'

'I haven't been able to think.'

'Moping about is always fatal. That's my advice, for what it's worth. Occupy yourself as much as you can.'

'Yes.'

'Are you returning to the school?'

'No.' My voice sounded firm. 'No.'

'It isn't my business,' said Mildred, 'but why not?'

'I can't. And I've no wish to. I shall never teach again.' I had decided.

'It's probably the strain —'

'No, Mother —'

'But, Ralph —'

'It's his life, Mary.'

'I suppose so.'

'No "suppose". It *is*.'

'Yes, Milly.'

'He has to fend for himself now.'

'Yes,' I said.

Mildred took the dishes to the kitchen.

'Being sharp is Milly's way.'

'Yes.'

'I would be lost without her.'

Mildred returned. She sat next to my mother on the sofa.

'How's your family?' I asked.

'What family?'

Her parents were dead, of course. 'Your brother.'

'You may or you may not remember, but I don't speak to my brother. I haven't seen him for many long years.'

'No, of course not.'

(No, of course not. Not since his wedding day. The band played loudly as Charlie – red-faced and drunk – walked across the dance floor and swayed in front of his sister. Billy Booth stood on one side of him; his new wife, Joyce, on the other. His right hand was behind his back. 'I've got something for you, Mildred, old fruit,' he said. Billy Booth smirked. Joyce giggled. 'What is it, Charlie?' Mildred asked. She smiled at her brother. 'You're the one for presents today, not me.' 'This is something very special, my old fruity, and it's just for you.' He suddenly produced a very thin, very long and very burnt sausage. 'I don't understand, Charlie.' 'You will, Mildred old fruit, you will. This is just what you need. It will solve all your problems.' He put it in her hands – 'Have a widow's memory, Milly. It will give you some nice ideas.' 'Stop it, Charlie,' said Mrs Harroway. 'Only a joke, Mum. The sooner she gets her hands round something long and hot, the better she'll be.' Mildred stood up. 'I shall never forgive you,' she said. She left the hall. 'It was only a joke,' said Billy. 'It was only a joke,' said Joyce.)

'I don't know why you asked about him, I'm sure.'

(Something to say. A topic for conversation.)

'I'm sorry.'

'No need to apologize.'

We sat in silence.

'I hope things will turn out better for you, Ralph.'

(Ralph. Ralph.)

'Thank you.'

'I wanted to say that to you, face to face, as it were.'

'Thank you.'

(Oh Lord, this yearning to be a child again, to place my head in her lap, to have her stroke my hair, gently, slowly. This yearning to have her speak my hated name: Ralphie. I actually want to hear it now, for the first time in my thirty years of life.)

Mildred takes my mother's hand in hers.

(I understand you as well as she does. I am learning about pain. I'm beginning.)

'Will you stay for tea?'

'No, Mother.'

(The old roses await me. That room's my province: nowhere else.)

I stood up.

'Well,' said my mother.

'Yes,' I said. 'Well.'

'It's goodbye then.'

'Goodbye, Mother.'

'Goodbye, Ralph.'

I lingered.

'Make your mind up, young man. Coming or going?'

'Going.'

'Then I'd use the hallway if I were you. It's the only way out.'

'Right. Goodbye.'

'Goodbye, Ralph.'

(Still Ralph.)

'Let's hope the rain holds off,' said Mildred. She closed the door behind me.

I boarded the train at Victoria.

There were faces opposite. I listened. Mouths opened and shut but no sounds came out. It is like a silent film of Babel, I thought, and I laughed at the very idea of such a thing.

A man was pressed against a woman. He touched her breast quickly and smiled. No one saw but me.

I turned to him as I left the train. 'That was Ernest Dinsdale's downfall,' I said.

The world through a mist: buildings, traffic, horrified faces. I used my knuckles as windscreen-wipers.

No sorrow, though, no reason.

I stood outside Mrs Ruby Dinsdale's house. I thought: I do not live here any more. I must find my way to my new room. I must get there quickly.

I got off the bus. Oh Christ, I thought, I'm still concerned what people think, I don't want them to see me in this state, I shall be embarrassed. As if it mattered. Mummy had brought up her Ralphie to be respectable, hadn't she? I stood still. I laughed.

I received a letter.

Since your visit yesterday [it began, without formalities] your mother has been in a state the like of which I have not seen her in for some years. She is as distressed as when your father died. You opened old scars. You may not have meant to but you did. Your mother feels things. It even hurt her when that woman your father nearly left her for died. I do not know why but there it is.

As your mother's best friend I think I have some cause to write to you. You left her alone and now you return. [She invited me! She wrote! You know she did, Mildred Harroway.] You have no idea of the upsets that result. It takes all I have to make her herself again. I do not complain, it is my lot in life, I would rather be with your mother than any other person. We are happy as two sandpipers most of the time.

I must get straight to the point. I am beating about the bush. I write this short message to ask you not to call on us again unless a case of emergency arises. Sickness or accident, God forbid. I ask you in all good faith. We are nearing the end, the two of us. It would be nice if whatever time is granted to us could be passed without hurts.

Have no fear. Your mother loves you. But it is me who cares for her. I am sorry about your wife. It would not be Christian of me to be otherwise. Of course I feel sorry for you. However we make our beds and we must lie on them.

M. HARROWAY

What did I say that opened old scars?

7

I brought my maze of words to an end. They had served their purpose. In and out of them, in and out, and only to discover – in a flash, in a sudden dart of light – that I had to be rid of my father's memory. How could I have loved, even revered, so remote a figure?

It was because he was remote, it was because he was a shadow, that I loved him so strongly. It is a difficult business loving flesh and blood. I had wanted my world brightened like some hopeless romantic.

And so had Ellie.

I have come to this with the aid of words.

Now I write down

THEN

and I am at work as I was that day. The class is assembled. We are going to read some scenes from *Julius Caesar*.

I allocate the parts: Davis, N., will play Cassius (he is tall and thin, anyway, and has a rasping voice); Nesbit, T., will make an adequate Brutus; Humber, P., whom the girls are in awe of, is everyone's obvious choice for Mark Antony; while June Pomeroy and Phyllis Oliffe will give strong support, as the saying goes, in the usually thankless roles of Calpurnia and Portia.

They begin to read. They are not convincing actors. They mistake commas for full stops and vice versa. Trevor Nesbit even reads the stage directions. There is nervous laughter from the back of the room.

We should read plays more often. They give me time to stare out of the window.

'Shall we read the next bit, sir?' a voice asks. They have come to the end of a scene. 'Yes. Go on until I tell you to stop.'

It is clear to me that Trevor Nesbit is a determined entertainer. 'Shout, Flourish,' he says loudly, his eyes on me. I share his look.

Later, when he sings 'Flourish and shout', the children laugh openly. I say nothing.

Slow and fat Morsman, F., who has been playing Caesar, obliges with groans as the knives sink into him. His death throes continue through several speeches. Someone applauds him.

Yawns greet the climax of P. Humber's oration. Clifford, M., gives Cinna the poet a pronounced lisp. When he announces that he is a bachelor, Trevor Nesbit whistles.

'Shall we go on, sir?'

'Why not?'

' "Act I – V –",' Trevor Nesbit says, ' "Scene One. Rome. A room in Antony's house. Enter Antony, Octavius and Lepidus." '

'Thank you, Nesbit.'

'That's all right, sir.'

There is a pause before Humber, P., as Antony, says ' "These many then shall die; their pricks are named." ' Humber, P., looks about him for support. The class is silent. He blushes.

But there is laughter when Smith, C., as Octavius, says ' "Prick him down, Antony." ' Humber, P., laughs loudest.

The girls, who have up to this point played the crowd, now adopt gruff voices for the soldiers. The name 'Titinius' is always announced with the stress on the first syllable.

Then I hear feet tramping. I stand up. It is not the children. I sit down. I turn my face to the light. The sun dazzles me. I look into it without blinking.

The feet are getting nearer. I count: One, two; one, two. It can only be soldiers.

It is. A horde of them. There are banners and bright helmets. Julius Caesar has a fat white face like Cousin Harry's. They are going to destroy, this horde, because the world is a senseless place. History is senseless. Effort is senseless. Only destruction is complete.

They loom above me. They break ranks. They charge. They are swift — I watch them as heads fall noiselessly to the floor — and they slice the desks in half in single strokes. Light bulbs drop from their sockets and smash.

I cannot watch such slaughter and not protest. I would not be human if I merely watched.

I rise, my hands gripping the sides of the table. My throat opens. Nothing. There *must* be a sound inside me.

I scream. I am human after all. I howl.

The echo stays with me.

It is over, everything quiet, the children before me like figures on a frieze. They come to life again with coughs and stares at each other and whispers. One boy smiles.

His name is Trevor Nesbit. His 'Lovers In The Sun' has been hanging on our kitchen wall for a long time.

HER

Her cure for every ill. 'I don't want to.' I walked out.

I went into a cinema and slept through a film which, I discovered on leaving, was called *A Thousand And One Lusts*.

Mrs Dinsdale crossed the hall as I entered the house. 'Good night, Mr Hicks.'

'Good night, Mrs Dinsdale.'

The room was in darkness. I turned on a lamp. The screen was on the floor in tatters. I picked it up and put it against my desk.

The note was on my ink-stand. 'Ralph. I would rather be dead than live with your contempt. I am sick with love of you. Elspeth.'

She was not in bed. She was not in the kitchen. 'Ellie,' I said. And then I shouted: 'Ellie. Ellie.'

I ran downstairs to the bathroom. The door was locked. 'Are you in there, Mr Korzeniowski?' I asked. I did not wait for his reply. I pushed and pushed. Finally, when I was near exhaustion, the door gave way.

She was by the bath. The taps were under her head. Like a pikestaff. There was blood on the wall and on the floor and on the lavatory seat.

I could not even mouth her name.

I tried to blink the red away. No use. I was drowning in it.

It stayed with me as I went down the stairs, eyes open or shut. It thickened with every step my feet took for me.

At last I saw, through the red I was drowning in, a darker shape. I stopped and it came towards me, largening, widening.

When it was near I clutched at it.

'Bath.'

The word miraculously out, the shape left my fingers and the floor was beneath me, smelling of lavender.

HERE

My doctor visited me this morning. He is younger than I am, which is strange.

He asked if I was progressing with my writing.

'Doctor,' I said, 'I want these fragments to speak for me. And for them.'

'For them?'

'The people I have had dealings with.'

'I see.'

'I want to look out now.'

'In that case,' he said, 'why don't we go for a walk?'

He seemed to be taking me literally, but I knew he knew what I meant.

We passed the apple tree. 'The birds get the apples before we do. They fall to the ground full of holes and rotting.'

We entered another building.

'Look in there,' he said. I stood beside him in the doorway. I saw a girl with wires attached to her head. 'Shock treatment.'

He invited me to look again and again. Blank faces. Dead eyes and open mouths. A man of seventy skipping, a woman with a dummy between her lips. A long ward of idiots laughing and dribbling.

My fellow ruins. My fellows.

I walked back to this room alone. I wept.

I end these fragments with a new word. I write down

MAN

in the hope that I will one day earn the right to use it about myself. My name is Ralph Hicks and I hope I will become a man. It is a beginning.